AT
THE SIGN OF THE
PHOENIX

Alexander Crombie

TSL Publications

First published in Great Britain in 2024
By TSL Publications, Rickmansworth

Copyright © 2024 Alexander Crombie

ISBN: 978-1-917426-07-7

Cover & photographs courtesy of :
https://pixabay.com/photos/manor-house-residence-property-3636256/
https://pixabay.com/vectors/crime-scene-dead-marks-person-body-30112/
https://pixabay.com/photos/owl-fire-flame-woman-fantasy-bird-1212930/
https://pixabay.com/photos/train-train-station-rail-japan-7819879/

Dedication

I dedicate this mainly fictional work to
Lieutenant Abbie Sweetwine, the "Angel of Platform 6."

Acknowledgements

I wish to thank the following people for their unique contributions to this book:--

David for sharing his firsthand experience of a traumatic event;

Christine for her valuable proofreading;

Anne Samson of TSL Publications for keeping the faith;

My wife Caroline for putting up with so many hours of the Author's solitary time at his keyboard; and

You my many loyal readers for embarking upon yet another adventure.

PROLOGUE I

London, 8 October 1952

Dense and evil smelling, the fog pushes relentlessly into the terminus of Euston station, as the girl battles her way through this Wednesday's rush hour.

For months now it has been her routine to travel to Watford each Saturday to get away from her husband, and to spend the day not with her sad and disappointed parents, but with her Godmother Evelyn. But this week the routine has to be broken at the urgent request of a work colleague needing to exchange her day off; and so the Saturday visit has been brought forward to Wednesday.

Auntie Evelyn, as she calls her Godmother, is only too happy to see her Godchild any time she can manage to get out of town, for she lives an isolated and house-bound existence. She is a person for whom life has receded. She has never married, preferring to respect the memory of her Scots fiancé, one of those thousands swallowed by Flanders' hungry maw in 1917.

In the years between, Evelyn has laboured for the Waifs and Strays Society, enduring the Blitz, and finally retiring on a minuscule pension.

Season ticket at the ready, the girl makes a beeline for her usual platform and the 8 a.m. express to Liverpool Lime Street which she is hoping and praying will stop at Watford Junction this day. She dodges and weaves through the oncoming flood of commuters, through heft and hustle of porters and gaggles of girls with hockey sticks, breathing in the while the nauseous fish breath of this cavern with its distorted soundscape thudding and echoing through her head. She begins to panic because the fog has disrupted the usual pace and rhythm of the capital and she is not sure she is going to make it to her train. Out of the corner of her eye she spots a display of gladioli at the flower stall. She breaks her step; does she have time to grab a bunch of the blooms for Evelyn? There are three customers in the queue, so she dashes on, grimacing at her reflection in the window of the ticket office.

At least she has this bulging bag of Victoria plums which she hopes will suffice in the place of flowers.

Waving her ticket in the face of the inspector, she makes it onto the platform as the guard is getting ready to hoist his green flag, while up ahead shuddering gouts of steam escape the double-headed locomotives of the Liverpool express.

The girl has been hoping to get aboard in or near to the kitchen car in the centre of the train, having had no time for her morning cup of tea. She is too late. Instead she is forced to make a dive for the last carriage as the whistle blasts in her ear and the train jerks into motion.

She tumbles rather than steps into the carriage, which is empty apart from a single passenger, a man, in the far corner. Barely she registers the man has a flop of blond hair, framed by heavy looking spectacles. He has his head buried in bundles of paperwork.

Quickly she gathers up her handbag along with the bag of plums – only a couple spilt – and slumps down to coil herself into the nearest window seat, praying that her fellow passenger will not look up to witness her blazing freckles and general air of dishevelment. A furtive glance in her compact mirror is reassuring, so she decides she will get on terms with the day by reading a chapter of *Vanity Fair* in the pocket edition given to her for her birthday by the same Aunt Evelyn.

She has her back to the engine as she prefers, and is feeling altogether more comfortable. She ventures a cautious half glance in the direction of her travelling companion, a youngish man it appears – tucked away in his corner seat; but as no answering glance comes her way, she finds her place in the book to pick up from where Becky Sharpe graduates from Miss Pinkerton's Academy For Young Ladies, contemptuously flinging away the gift of Johnson's *Dictionary*. "How could you do that?" Becky's friend Emelia chides her companion. But the girl is not destined to read Becky Sharpe's reply for more than twenty years, because in an endless moment the world, her world, splinters and explodes in heart stopping violence and chaos.

PROLOGUE II

Six Months Earlier

Leo Church, school master by profession, bachelor by default, and dedicated follower of footpaths, was not normally a man to leave things to chance, and he allowed only one exception to this rule.

Sniffing with relish at the fresh spring air of the West Country market place, he fished out his lucky coin. "Heads" and he would go north; "Tails!" and he would head south.

With a sturdy flick the coin flew high, flashed brightly, tumbled, and came down "Tails." Leo's decision was made for him; the unforeseen consequences would follow soon enough.

Back an hour and Leo was happily ensconced in the breakfast room of the Fletchers Arms. Well into the holiday spirit and reminding himself, "Today's your birthday," he had nothing more serious to think about than whether to have an extra sausage with his "Full-English," and whether to wear his shorts. He decided "Yes" to both.

The old coaching inn was quiet for the time of year, but looking up from his toast and Oxford marmalade Leo noticed "Mary and Joseph" in the far corner of the room, their heads bowed together. For his own amusement he had christened the young couple "Mary" and "Joseph" the previous evening when following them into the Fletchers. It was the sling hoisted high on the boy's back with its hooded burden which could only be a baby that had put the idea into his head.

Joseph was tallish, loose-limbed, rather bowed around the shoulders. A smallish face with simian eyes was topped by an overflowing mass of dark curls.

Abruptly Joseph got up and sidled out of the room. Despite himself, Leo looked over to where Mary sat apathetically sipping at her coffee. She presented a fairer picture with long straw-coloured hair and large light-blue eyes. She wore no make-up and, as far as Leo could see, no ring or other indications of matrimony.

Some minutes later and by chance, Leo found he was leaving the dining room at the same moment as Mary. Heading for the stairs, Mary seemed to change her mind for some reason, and the two collided, the girl dropping her bag. With a smart "My fault, allow me," Leo scooped up the bag, presenting it to the girl with a sketched salute, barely acknowledged by the girl. The touch of hands had been almost non-existent.

* * *

If Leo felt any disappointment at the failure of his small act of gallantry, this was very soon banished by the brilliant promise of the day. First there was the town to rediscover after some years of absence. Glory be! Leo found that the Copper Kettle Tearoom was still going strong. He was pretty sure he recognised the proprietress whose figure struck him as the perfect advertisement for her home-made cakes – had food rationing ever got this far, he wondered. The flapjack, moist and aromatic, was recalled with relish, and he crammed four pieces into his rucksack. Then, pausing only to copy the details of an ancient plaque into his notebook, he brandished his ash plant and bustled his way out of town, his short jerky stride reminiscent of the padded wicket-keeper that once had been "Church Ma."

Leo's route took him across the deer-park down to a splendidly wide and ancient oak and thence over a busy little brook lined by pungent banks of wild garlic.

The day delighted. On past birthdays he had been used to eking out the hours of daylight in the tranquil company of his widowed mother, who however was distant from his thoughts this anniversary. If anyone threatened to be on Leo's mind, it was Jasper Earlham-Jones, his Sixth Form nemesis; yet even EJ and his machinations were banished by sunshine and wine-rich Cotswold air.

As the track climbed away from the brook, Leo came face to face with a gnarled nut of a man in the act of aiming a heavy mallet at a hole. At the bottom of the hole that Leo automatically looked into – because holes are there to be looked into – he spied sturdy cross-struts anchoring a new Waymark post. The two men exchanged knowing looks as much as to say,

"The vandals won't shift this one once it's been back-filled!" But without a word Leo nodded deferentially and strode on.

The track was good and well maintained, a match for Leo's energetic stride. As he went he hummed something from Gilbert & Sullivan, glorying in the clean vigour of the day and the dappling of the greenwood. He was not distracted by thoughts of vandalism; he was certainly not preoccupied by the state of the teaching profession with its hidebound practitioners and its young criminals in the making. There were times when he bemoaned the fading of respect for his ancient profession, but today was not one of those times, and to prove it and without breaking stride he swung the ash plant through the head of a rangy wayside thistle.

There was an Iron Age fort a couple of hills further on, which Leo remembered from the last time he had walked this way. He thought he would stop at the fort for an early picnic. Cresting the intervening hill, he slowed his stride, not so much to recover his breath, as to admire the crumbling remains of the fort crouching over the valley a mile off. Imagination took over. The rude but resourceful men who had built their fortification certainly knew how to pick their spot. He pictured their foes attempting a frontal assault from any point of the compass, and could not suppress a shiver of *schadenfreude*.

Lowering his gaze Leo spotted two figures crawling towards the fort and ... yes ... they had to be Mary and Joseph. They were half a mile from where he stood, but the baby bobbing on the boy's back gave them away. It would be pleasant, he thought to catch them up and perhaps offer them something from his picnic. So, with best-foot-forwards he plunged on down the track.

As it turned out, the rendezvous proved timely. A hundred yards or so below the fort Leo saw that the young couple were struggling to open a five-barred gate while looking apprehensively over their shoulders at an encircling posse of cattle.

"Hello there!" Leo made his greeting sound as relaxed and confident as possible.

Mary and Joseph stared back with blank faces. "Poor things," Leo thought, "They're on their honeymoon ... Couldn't afford one at the time ... Natural habitat the back-streets of Brum ... Encountering 'the perils' of the countryside for the first time."

With raised voice he called out to them, "Don't worry, they're only cows, I promise you. Just that they've got their calves with them so that makes them a bit protective."

Still not convinced, the couple shrank back against the gate, so Leo strode forward in shooing-mode, and the beasts backed off.

"Morning to you!" Leo was up with them now. "Must say, that little baby of yours would seem to be the coolest member of the party! Mind if I introduce myself?"

Without waiting for an answer Leo twitched back the hood atop the sling on Joseph's back. What he saw then jerked Leo backwards as if he had been stung by electricity. The "baby" was not a baby at all but a doll, and not any ordinary doll but a hideous grotesque, a parody of a girl-child with venomous staring eyes and arrows of red and black crisscrossing the obscenely bulging cheeks.

The silence was broken by Joseph. "That's Mattie. Keeps away the bad spirits does Mattie."

"Doesn't do so well with cows," Leo finally muttered through clenched teeth.

Nonplussed, Leo tried to catch the girl's eye, not ready to believe that she would go in for such a horror, such a travesty of infant-kind even if the boy did; but Mary looked away, face devoid of life or expression.

For lack of anything else to say, Leo asked the boy, "You two on your way south then?"

Joseph seemed to consider this for a moment before replying, "There's a gathering down there tonight, see?" Vaguely he pointed over the hill. "Then we're off to The Stones."

With the uneasy feeling that his bright, all-right-with-the-world day was crumbling around him, Leo abruptly vaulted the gate, turning a stern face back at the couple. "I trust the organiser of your hmm gathering has been to the Authorities for the appropriate permission? There is such a thing as trespass you know."

"Might have." This time the voice was stronger, the gaze more focused. "Anyways, my girlfriend and me, we've got a little bit of business with yo."

Leo stared back at the boy through the bars of the gate. "I doubt that very much. What business could you possibly have with me?" And he speared the turf with his stick by way of emphasis.

"Back along there," Joseph jabbed a finger over his shoulder, "you made a pass at my girlfriend, didn't you. After breakfast you had a good grope, didn't you. And she didn't like it, and we think that'll have to cost you – we was thinking a hundred quid – or we'll just have to tell your snooty friends all about it. That right Doll?"

Mary kept her gaze fixed on the distant Black Mountains, but nodded imperceptibly.

Leo hardly knew whether to laugh or to explode with rage. No one had remotely spoken to him like that since as an over-enthusiastic schoolboy scrum-half he'd been taken to task for committing repeated off-sides.

For a moment he glared stonily down at the boy from the rising ground on his side of the gate. Then turning away he threw over his shoulder, "You can both go to hell and take that monstrosity with you!"

Bypassing the fort Leo strode away at a quick-march across the fall line. Once he looked back to see the couple still struggling to untie the gate.

A furious mile further and he was in the heart of an ancient village, a pint of Real Ale to his dried lips. Trying hard to recover the innocent magic of the morning he sighed, musing ruefully, "Leo Church, do you realise it's your twenty-fifth birthday and you've yet to do anything for which you could be blackmailed, well not really."

With another deeper sigh he drained his pot, hefted rucksack, grasped his ash plant and set his face to the south.

PART I

Leo, 1927 – 1946

Leo has never said much about his father, perhaps because he never knew him in the flesh. It seems that Gordon Church was a railway man, a one-career man, dedicated and driven. Years before the arrival of a nationally owned transport system, Gordon was a guard on LMS, the London Midland and Scottish company. As a servant of this prestigious operation he worked the longest possible hours until one December morning of fog and disruption to the network, he died. Seven months later Leo was born.

Leo's mother Catriona-Jean, known as Jeanie, was and remained a woman of character. Born in Dingwall in the Scottish Highlands in the final decade of Queen Victoria's reign, she emerged from the day by day rigours and hardships of the fishing community to put herself through a nurse's training course in Glasgow. There by chance she worked as a probationer under Ward Sister Drummond. Again by chance – for Sister Drummond was sparing with any talk that did not relate strictly to the care of her ward – the women soon discovered their ancestors had each been victim of the highland clearances that had forced the crofters off their lands in the middle of the eighteenth century. The migration that followed that crime had led to years of grinding poverty, but had added tensile steel to bred in the bone endurance.

"Tensile" yes. The steel proved pliant as Jeanie completed training and on the recommendation of Sister Drummond she moved all the way to London Town to embark on her full time career at Saint Bartholomew's Hospital. There and still only eighteen, Jeanie was in time to join in receiving the deluge of casualties that poured into Waterloo Station following the German Spring Offensive in Picardy. And one of those many casualties arriving cased in yards of soiled bandages was a young West Country lad, Gordon Church.

By itself the shrapnel that had sliced through Gordon's leg would not have proved fatal. What was more threatening was the ever-present danger of sepsis setting in to poison the blood. Much had been learned over the war years about the effects of sepsis and related pathologies such as gangrene, and in Gordon's case urgent treatment and nursing by Jeanie and her fellows saved a life.

War's end saw Gordon discharged from hospital with two things. One was a small but pronounced limp to the left leg; the other was a hastily scrawled note of Jeanie's address at the nurses' home.

In the quaint language of those days Gordon and Jeanie walked out together. Strolls through Hyde Park refreshed by lemonade and penny buns were interspersed with an outing to the theatre to see *Pineapple Poll,* and visits to the East End to see Marie Lloyd and her fellow icons performing in music hall, where oranges and nuts enhanced the experience. Gordon was demobilised from the army, and to celebrate took Jeanie down to the Wye Valley to be introduced to his hop and apple farming family.

The courtship lasted for all of four years while Gordon established his career on the railways, and Jeanie steadily rose in seniority in her nursing career. Patience was something that came naturally to each of them, for life was all to do with saving up as pennies painstakingly turned into pounds. But eventually Gordon judged they were able financially to marry. In his home village the avenues of plane trees were just coming into leaf. The timing felt right.

The wedding was unusual in that it took place not in the bride's home parish but in an ancient village church some dozen miles from the county town of Gordon's home shire. The service was conducted according to the rites of the established Church of England, and was blessed by sunshine from morning to evening. In the years to come, Leo would often gaze at his parents' wedding photograph, just the one back in those days, in the hope of divining truths about his parents and especially his father. In the country of apples it was not surprising that blossoms were all around, in the bridegroom's lapel and in the bride's bouquet. Peering nervously into the sun, Gordon faced the camera, not hiding a certain weakness of jaw. For her part Jeanie was caught side face, head raised to smile at her newly minted husband, resolution imprinted on eyes and mouth.

Forming a shallow semi-circle behind the bridal couple were Gordon's parents, beaming extravagantly, together with the rest of his close relations. Jeanie's widowed mother was not present, arthritis preventing her from assaying the lengthy journey south. In her place her family was represented by Jeanie's Uncle Murray; Murray Watt who presented a bold figure stood a step back from his niece. Though seldom venturing south of the Tweed, this uncle was to play an important role in affairs to come.

* * *

In most things Jeanie was a practical rational woman, in mind as well as action. This was proved by the stoical fashion by which she seemed to accept and recover from the early death of her husband and the birth of their son. Yet there proved an exception to this. Understanding the birth was likely to be in the first half of August, Jeanie settled early on Leo as the baby's given name. Whether this impulse owed anything to the workings of her Gallic genes would never be known. What she did admit to was a belief that as a child to be born under the sign of Leo her child might expect to be confident and ambitious of character, thoroughly fitted for life with all its demands and imperatives. But as matters panned out the baby was to be born early and under the sign, not of Leo but, of Cancer the crab. That meant according to Jeanie's lexicon that her child was likely to be caring, inquisitive, charismatic and loyal, but also possessive, moody, secretive, and demanding of loyalty.

It will not add to the story of Leo's early life to relate infantile ailments, the success or failure of his fourth birthday celebrations, or the progression of his early education. Apart from the tireless and selfless devotion of his mother Jeanie, two matters of breeding stood out.

The first of these concerned the Scotsman uncle, Murray Watt. At an early age Murray had broken away from the fishing communities of the far north-west to educate himself in Scotland's capital city and to gain qualification as a Writer To The Signet, the Scottish equivalent to a solicitor. At the cost of a modest premium he proceeded to buy himself into a highly reputable practice of lawyers in the same city, for whom he disposed his considerable knowledge of private trusts. Though far from a demonstrative man, the bachelor Watt soon endeared himself to his clients for the balance of his mind and the forward thinking of his advice. He never rushed those advices, preferring as one of his fellow lawyers once observed, "To take each word out and look at it before uttering."

Having served due notice of his intention through the mails, Murray Watt took the long road south to closet himself with his niece one weekend during the spring preceding Leo's eighth birthday. Of course he had an agenda. Murray's single agenda related to Leo's future education, and was not intended to call for any subsequent pilgrimages, and nor were there to prove more than one in the years following.

Ensconced on the rustic bench that looked out over Jeanie's cottage garden, the lawyer started with a few exchanges with Leo himself. Not especially easy around children, Murray went to some pains to avoid their conversation sounding stilted, and by degrees he won the confidence of the boy to ferret out a variety of facts germane to his visit. When Leo finally asked if it was all right to go, the lawyer summoned a smile and nodded his consent.

Next it was Jeanie's turn. After quizzing his niece about her earnings and her items of expenditure, Murray inclined his head by way of acknowledge-ment, pausing to jot down notes with a gold-tipped fountain pen. He then half turned to look directly at Jeanie sat arms folded at the opposite end of the bench. With a clearing of the throat he launched into what he had come all those miles to discuss. "My dear, there is nothing I am saying that I have not already approached with your mother who is fully in agreement that our meeting take place." He paused for a moment to tuck a wing of pepper and salt hair behind his ears. "So, I have now had the benefit of seeing you and young Leo in, shall we say, your natural habitat. Two things are clear to me. Number one, the boy is bright and deserves the best education available to him. Number two, there exists a strong bond between the two of you which I am confident will not be prejudiced whatever decision we may come to."

Aware that her uncle had more to say, Jeanie kept her mouth resolutely shut, but levelled her jaw, keeping eye contact with the lawyer. Murray continued, "In short your mother and I would like to see young Leo attend a boarding school to develop his finer qualities. Owing to certain researches I have undertaken I am able to recommend an academy not so many miles from here, which I believe will fit the bill admirably."

Seeing that Jeanie was about to react, possibly to bridle, he raised a placating hand. "My dear, I think I may know what may be on your mind.

The boy will not need to feel estranged from what is clearly an excellent home and home life. The college I have in mind has exeats twice in every term, and of course the holidays are far from short. Then there is the matter of fees, and here I hope I can be the bearer of good news. Across and on my side of the Tweed there exists a trust, a family trust – please note I did not say "charitable trust" – which can be drawn upon to cover fees and incidentals. While I am sure that you will wish to contribute towards the overall cost out of your steady earnings and your late husband's railway pension, small though that is, I can assure you I have already costed the whole project and have got the account to balance."

Jeanie thought for several moments. "If we were back home, I mean, in Scotland, I know Leo would have his pick of excellent grammar schools where he could be a day-boy, maybe get a scholarship. I cannot deny, losing Leo to a life of boarding will be a hard pill to swallow, whatever the advantages may be."

"You are right to say this, Jeanie, and I would not be suggesting the plan if I did not think it would be in yon laddy's best interests. But having sprung it on you so to speak, I have no wish to hurry your decision because that is what it is, your decision. I am going to take myself off to that fair looking hostelry in yon village and return if I may tomorrow to answer your questions and to see if we can come to a decision."

The second matter of breeding came to the surface as Leo settled into life at Merelles Academy following his mother's decision to go with her uncle's plan. In the years to come, Jeanie would reflect on just how closely her son's character took on the qualities of that zodiacal sign. On the one hand his confidence proved a tender plant that grew slowly, needing steady reassurance. As for ambition, this was entirely lacking.

On the other hand, Leo's end of term reports spoke of "Steadiness, loyalty," and "Intuitive as well as rational thinking." Ever watchful, Jeanie would add, "secretive moody and just a little bit possessive." The one area where there was no lack of agreement was loyalty and the expectation of loyalty in return.

As Leo progressed up the school, graduating from the prep department into the seniors, his burgeoning personality best expressed itself on the cricket field. An attacking batsman he was not; a game-changing bowler he was not. Leo found his perfect niche behind the stumps as wicket-keeper, never flashy but always dependable. In terms to be fashionable in later years, he was "reactive" rather than "proactive." On his own he was never going to win a game for his school, whereas he could lose a game by dropping a catch or letting through too many byes.

While he judged it unnecessary to journey south more than once during his great nephew's school career, Murray Watt regularly had forwarded to him Leo's school reports as well as the termly accounts. As the boy reached Sixth Form Murray wrote to Jeanie about the advantages of a career in the law; though when word got back that Leo felt school mastering was more likely to prove his bent, the lawyer declined to force the issue. And so it was that LG Church was gratefully accepted on to the staff of Merelles without intermediate qualification of any sort. Staff ranks were depleted due to the war and the demands of HM Forces; and besides, there would be time enough to garner letters after his name.

Leo, June 1946

Reluctantly Leo Church looked up from his marking to see "Spider" Williams sidling up towards the dais. The scene was Detention Room 3 in the old wing of Merelles Academy in the heart of a far from merry England. The need Merelles had for not one but three detention rooms spoke volumes about the rigour of its discipline; though on this occasion, nearing the end of the Summer Term, Leo was custodian to just the one detainee.

The air of early evening was heavy with the pungent savour of newly mown grass blended with chalk dust and orange peel, so that Leo's head swam. From outside raucous volleys of cheering reminded the young school master that the First Eleven were engaged in their annual contest – some called it a "grudge match" against their old enemies from across the county, and he would have given almost anything to be sat in the pavilion, if only as assistant scorer. Instead of that, what he had was Spider Williams.

Leo had no idea what Spider's given name was. He had not the slightest interest in finding out; besides which the chaps had no use for first names, habitually referring to themselves as "Cavendish" or "Beauchamp" or even "Smith". Vaguely it registered with Leo that Spider, a boy from the Lower Fourth, had got his nickname from something he was fond of parroting in the faces of all-comers and apropos of nothing at all. Now as he shifted his marking to one side and sighing deeply, he realised he was about to be Spider's latest target.

"Excuse me Sir, but would you rather be a spoider or a fly?" Yes, as Leo had once overheard in passing, "spoider" definitely had a West Country ring to it, rendering it no ordinary "spider" in Williams's lexicon.

Leo was tempted to dismiss the boy, send him packing back to his desk and the copying out of punishment lines. Yet his marking was all but completed, and he was bored. "You mean Williams I have to make a choice? Because I'm really not interested in being either a spider or a fly."

The boy craned his neck a little the better to achieve a fraction of eye contact with the master of the dais. His expression of guileless innocence was somewhat undermined by the sweat on his upper lip and the riot of spots spreading to either side of his mouth. When he spoke his tone was wheedling. "But Sir, everyone's either a spoider or a fly. I only wanted to know which you would prefer to be."

Leo reached a finger to his neck to ease the grip of his collar. "So tell me Williams, delve as far as you're able into your tiny mind and tell me, is this 'spider and fly' business something of classical literature that's landed in your apology for a brain? Something perhaps suggested by the great Socrates, or maybe it's Aesop and his fables that's inspired you, no?"

The boy's face took on a perplexed look. In response to his mantra he was used to receiving a slap or two in the face from his contemporaries, followed sometimes by an excruciating Half-Nelson. He was not used to trading esoteric niceties. "That's all right Sir. I'll put you down as a spoider." With which he ducked his head and trailed back to his seat and the writing of lines.

The remaining ten minutes of detention inched by while a lone fly investigated a pool of watery goo along the windowsill. Finally the period bell shrilled and each captive instantly relaxed to the urgent prospect of freedom.

Leo had no further duties ahead of lights-out in the dormitories, so for a look at the cricket he strolled in the direction of the terrace by way of the cloister with its portrait gallery of Officer Training Corps boys.

The terrace was a favourite spot. It faced to the west which meant that Leo had to squint to follow the progress of the match; yet it was obvious that Merelles were coasting to victory, so that he was unashamed to find a spare deck-chair and to rest his eyes for a few minutes.

In his mind's eye he could visualise the entire campus of the school that had been his surrogate home since the age of eight. At his back there ranged the bulk of the school's buildings standing out proudly in their blood red brick. Constructed along a low ridge these buildings, "Big School", "Little School", the chapel, the sanatorium and most of the classrooms looked down over much of the hundred acre site. Without opening an eye Leo could pinpoint the athletics field, the Firsts, Seconds and Colts cricket pitches, the open-air swimming pool, the Fives courts and of course the armoury. This last, equipped as it was with its state-of-the-art rifle range, was always first in line to be shown off to visitors from the military and Ministry of Defence by a proud, even unctuous Headman.

As one of the bachelor masters, Leo lived inside the college. His accommodation was a single bed sitting-room perched high in one of the towers that flanked the main entrance. This lofty fastness boasted no facilities for bathing or moving of the bowels for which he was obliged to forage with the boys for use of their bathrooms. The only advantage of this meagre accommodation was his view from the semi-circular windows, one looking west over the playing fields and the other pointing in the opposite direction down the long drive leading from an imperious set of wrought iron gates which marked the boundary of college grounds.

As for the furnishing of Leo's turret room, this was sparse. Apart from the single bed, there was a makeshift wardrobe, a small keyhole desk and a single hard-back chair. As he was used to nothing more lavish, Leo got along with the spartan condition of his home well enough, finding a corner of the wardrobe for his kettle and his biscuit tin and devoting one of his windowsills to his photographs, one of the battleship HMS *Vanguard*, the other smaller print, that of his mother.

Visitors were rare. When the occasional visitor tracked him down to his lofty lair he – for it was always a he – had no choice but to perch on the bed while Leo squeezed past to put the kettle on to boil. The most regular visitor was Will Piper. Another of the bachelor masters, Will was two or three years Leo's senior and so had seen active service in the last year of the war, albeit on a "hostilities-only" commission. Leo for his part had narrowly escaped call-up to HM Armed Forces due to the fall of his birthday, and for the same reason had avoided the lottery of going down the mines as a Bevin Boy.*

At first meeting the two young masters had hit it off together. Reminding Leo a bit of David Copperfield's meeting up with Steerforth, Will had leadership bred in the bone, and was good at rallying his friend if for any reason he felt down. More than once he had hastened to Leo's side when a dormitory riot threatened to get out of hand. And there was also the home thing. Will's people lived in a converted oast house in the depths of Herefordshire hop country, not a million miles from Leo's own home, so

---

* Wartime demands on the drafting of servicemen led to loss of vital labour in the country's coal mines. In 1944 HM government introduced the compulsory drafting to the mines of every tenth man eligible for call-up to the forces. The tenth boy was known as a "Bevin Boy" after the name of the government minister who introduced the scheme.

that they had been able to meet up occasionally during the long college vacations.

Will Piper was not the only master back from the war. CBW Dance, known to his contemporaries as "CB" was older, having taught music at Merelles over a decade, before gaining a commission and joining a Guards regiment in 1939. Another bachelor, CB was back where people felt he belonged, teaching from morning to night with the expression of a bloodhound in search of quarry. Dance's tragedy however was his loss of hearing in one ear, the result of a shell splinter sustained during the battle for Caen, which had also left a livid legacy in the shape of a partly collapsed right jaw. The fear that this disfigurement induced in younger pupils was unfortunately magnified by his relish for caning. If a boy was summoned to CB's room for running in the cloisters or laughing out of turn in one of his classes, that boy knew what he was in for. He was required to bend over the master's piano stool and wait while CB took his time to choose a suitable cane. Punishment carried out, CB expected the boy to stand tall and shake hands.

Herbert Cantevill was Merelles' Second Master. Answering only to his surname, Cantevill had been at the college man and boy for most of his long life, leaving only to gain a Masters degree in Classics from one of the older universities. Short and barrel-shaped he was never seen without gown and mortarboard, and a withering look for anyone he considered inappropriately or sloppily dressed. In an important sense Cantevill could be said to run Merelles as it was he who set the College's timetable with pride and precision. His power of recall was just as impressive, enabling him to bring to mind Old Merellesians fallen as far back as in the Great War.

Physical training at Merelles was in the rigorous hands of Sergeant Bloxham. Bloxham, he of the balding head and simian features, ruled his domain without benefit of mirth or mercy. Any boy who escaped the Sergeant's judgement "miserable specimen" could truthfully feel he had won first prize in life's lottery. Not a natural athlete himself, Leo Church preferred to give Bloxham, as well as his more sporty colleagues somewhat of a wide birth.

* * *

That year Merelles' head boy was Jasper Earlham-Jones. "Jaz" to Maxwell and Gladwin and the rest of his honoured inner circle, and "The Earl," to the "vermin" of lower down the school, Earlham-Jones gloried in his status. Dark and sharp of feature with hair bryl-creamed a la Dennis Compton, EJ loved nothing more than to hold court. The court was the western terrace, and the members of the court apart from Maxwell and Gladwin consisted of much of the rugby and cricketing Firsts. Not that the Earl stooped to muddying his knees; rather, he preferred to demonstrate how a break from the scrum might be best achieved or a cover drive executed. His one official role would find him in immaculate white coat and panama hat, umpiring the Colts.

EJ was the product of new money. His "People," as he was wont to refer to his parents, were snugly arrived in a leafy enclave of Surrey. His father born Ron Earl in Hornchurch, had enjoyed a good war. From selling American imported nylon stockings on markets all round the capital, Pa Earl had graduated to riskier merchandising. By this time he could afford to outsource much of his business activities so that the stain of black marketeering never quite stuck, close as that might have been at times. And besides, had anyone come out in public with a direct accusation, he now had the cash as well as the self-confidence to threaten legal action.

Then in the last year of the war EJ's Pa had become one hundred percent legit. As well as landing himself a succession of lucrative contracts to dispose of surplus defence equipment such as airfields, he explored a burgeoning talent for political networking. As he was to tell his son repeatedly, "My Boy, you must always have a speciality in life." Ronald Earl's speciality was exchange control in all of its intricate windings. Thus in influential circles the end of hostilities marked him out as a "Coming Man." And by way of a simple deed poll he equipped himself for the future by losing the "Ron Earl" in favour of "Ronald Earlham-Jones."

Of EJ's birth mother and his father's first wife, there is nothing that can be said, as Leo never found out anything about her. All that is known is that Pa Earlham-Jones surreptitiously divested himself of the lady sometime early in the war to marry Gloria in her place. It is doubtful that Leo would ever have met Gloria, but it seems the lady, product of a minor county family from the South Coast, proved to be all that Earlham-Jones senior could aspire to, both in bed and out. As for relations between EJ and his step-mother, conjecture there is none.

Leo Church's contacts with EJ were few and intermittent. There was nothing surprising about that. As the most junior of junior masters Leo's roles kept him away from the exalted realm of the Upper Sixth as well as "seniors" sporting activities. All the same he could not help but be aware of "The Earl."

For one thing, suppress the feeling though he might, he was only too conscious that he was barely a year older than the Head Boy. In the normal way of things Leo was not likely to be called upon to discipline EJ for infringement, major or minor, of college rules. For one thing EJ's habitual stance shouted to the world, "I'm the chap in charge around here. Rules are no concern of mine." This air of arrogance still got to Leo. The way that EJ adopted his studied saunter across the terrace and the way he had of dismissing ash from the end of his cigar, itched at a burgeoning resentment. It was something he occasionally spoke about with Will, his friend Will Piper. So it was in Will that Leo confided after a clash occurred. "I was doing nothing more officious than trying to hurry a group of lads into chapel last Sunday evening. Earlham-Jones clearly felt the need to finish his cigar* and was not to be rushed. So what did he do, he pointedly stepped in front of me, blew smoke in my face and out of nowhere accused me of dodging the call-up in favour of a cushy number in school mastering!" With those two additional years of experience and maturity Will waved the matter out of the window of the turret room. "Forget it old chap, it's all a juvenile pose. Don't you dare react." But then the day came when there was no choice but to react to a dramatic event.

It was one week from the end of the term and the end of the school year. Examinations were gathered in, and the boys were at a loose end, not wholly in one world or another. It was not just hot, it was stifling, and discipline in the dorms was all but broken down.

Leo approached the Upper Fourth's dorm with reluctance. Asking why he could hear so much noise he was told that no one could sleep and, "May we have another window open, Sir?"

Noting that two of the larger windows gaped open wide, Leo wanted to know what was wrong with the smaller window set into the gable end. On being told it was stuck fast he clambered on to a chair and managed with some effort to dislodge and open wide the sash. At this point his head protruded a foot or so outside so that his gaze travelled down the steep drop

---

* At Merelles smoking of tobacco was permitted for Sixth Formers in their final term.

to the sheltered yard outside the school's laundry. What Leo saw down there meant that his head did not at once retreat into the dorm.

What Leo glimpsed three floors down could not possibly be misunderstood. Vaguely he thought the girl's name was Daisy. If indeed it was the young laundry maid Daisy, Daisy was standing backed up against the wall of her work place. She was not moving, she was not really able to move because pinning her with both arms was Head Boy Jasper Earlham-Jones.

Leo's head ducked out again. He had to make sure he was not seeing things. He was not. As he craned his head downwards he could see that the first embrace might have been to the girl's liking, while the boy's grappling attempt to remove her blouse clearly was not. Leo clattered the sash down, intending the clatter to be heard below. One of the dorm boys – was it Spider Williams – wanted to know what the master had been looking at. "Nothing to interest you, Williams. Just a bit of unusual ornithology."

Leo fled the dorm to race down three flights of stairs and end up outside the laundry. The courtyard was empty. He tracked down Earlham-Jones on the terrace, posing nonchalantly, the first whiff of smoke curling from a large cigar. Despite protest the boy was marched to the resident house master's rooms. There he stood defiantly, hands behind his back, while Leo recited the charge. The master who had been dragged away from a table of contract Bridge, looked less than interested in the recital. "Well Earlham-Jones, what have you got to say for yourself?"

The boy blustered. "Sir, you must know those laundry girls, always looking for a bit of, hmm, slap and tickle."

The master raised his eyes to the ceiling. He declined to look either at Leo or at Earlham-Jones. "Young man, temptation exists to be resisted. In one week's time you will be free to go your own way. Until then you will kindly spare me further reference to, hmm, the laundry. Dismiss."

Beth

Her spine is pinned to the bulkhead, compressed by the violence of unearthly impact. Another split second and her body knifes into a ball. A moment in which the clash of opposing forces balances on a splinter of time, and the ball fires itself to the opposite side of the compartment where it collapses like a rag doll to a crescendo of tearing metal and flying fabric. A mere fraction of awareness barely glimpsed through the rolling detonation, follows in the wake of her body's projectile. There is no reason here, only the acceptance that this is death.

She forces one eye to open. She is in a realm of fog. Dense clouds of dust and grit shroud the place where the window should be ... But she can see; she can see, but she cannot hear. There is still sound, yet it seems to be reaching her from a great distance as if she is plunged beneath fathoms of water. A beginning of focus edges back to her senses. The man with the out-sized glasses lies sprawled across the wreckage of the seats. Obscurely she drags herself to the thought that he is someone she has last seen in another life, another existence. Dimly her brain inches towards a connection ... but the man's head is wreathed in blood, and how can she possibly do anything about that? There is nothing she can do about that ... she is just too tired ... She loses consciousness.

A moment that might be a minute and a fragile glint of awareness swims back so that she finds herself again staring at the man. The glasses are mashed into his face. One lens is intact, but the other pokes out from his eye at a jagged angle. She tries to stand, to go to the man, but her body will not obey. She collapses and again loses consciousness. When her mind comes back to her she is aware of sinewy arms hoisting her through the air. She allows her limbs to go limp, her whole body to surrender.

* * *

Beth Tringham was born on Christmas Day 1930, ten minutes after the family returned home from Midnight Mass. It was fortunate that both the doctor and the midwife were each congregated that ice-bound holy night, as a panicky journey to the cottage hospital would have been no light undertaking.

The church in question was dedicated to St Jude, and stood on a swell of land overlooking the village, surrounded by its graveyard in which five generations of Tringhams lay at rest. The venerable building had stood there for eight hundred years reminding parishioners of its presence by the thrice daily tolling of its tenor bell, while announcing a death by means of the passing toll.

Girdling the maypole at its centre, the village spread itself in a rough semi-circle. Below the Green stood the Home Farm with its ramshackle sheds and stack yards. On either side of the Green and stretching up towards St Jude's, ancient huddles of alms houses crouched higgledy piggledy. To the east of Home Farm fields stretched away into the distance, some still retaining the humps and hollows denoting the agriculture of medieval times. At the top end of the village, flanked by a number of half-timbered houses, a broad avenue of pollarded limes led off the Otford road to the Manor House, home of the Tringham family. All around, the land of the Kentish Men.

Proud of their lineage as Kentish Men, superior to those Men of Kent over to the east, the Tringhams could trace their ancestry as far back as the Stewart kings and beyond into the mists of history. A portrait hung in the gallery of the Manor House depicting the heavily bearded figure of William Tringham who, family legend would have one believe, had fought alongside Churchill Duke of Marlborough at the battle of Blenheim in the Low Countries. Nothing was now recalled as to how William had acquitted himself against the Frenchies, whether he had suffered wounds, whether he had had one or more horses shot from under him. All the same his portrait had been worth its fee, so it was believed by his descendants that at the very least he had not cut and run.

Of the Tringhams who followed William even less was known, although a rumour persisted that Beth's great grandfather might have been a remittance man, dispatched with a regular allowance far from Britannia's shores to relieve the family of taint from his drinking, his gambling, or something else unspeakable, ungentlemanly. In any event the gallery displayed no portraits between that of William and that of Beth's grandfather Rufus.

Clean shaven and with a hawkish cast of face, Rufus had inherited the Tringham lands back in the 80s. He for certain had been more of an adventurer than a farmer; yet he had had the knack of making more money than he dispensed, so that the estate prospered over his lifetime. A reserve officer in a fashionable regiment, he was well regarded by people who mattered in society, a fact that came close to making his name for him. In the family archive there was retained a letter, a personal letter from Henry Morton Stanley enquiring as to whether Rufus might be available to join the explorer and saviour of the sainted Doctor Livingstone in a mission to rescue a stranded colonialist from Africa's dark heart. The invitation had not been taken up for the simple reason that Rufus had been in Argentina at the time, prospecting for beef cattle. Subsequently Rufus had been too old to fight in the war against Germany, but had perished in the pandemic of Spanish Flu immediately following the end of hostilities. It followed that Beth had never known this grandfather.

Beth's own father, Sidney Tringham, had been born on the very last day of Victoria's reign, a coincidence that tended to restrain the celebration of his arrival on account of the nation's mourning, with the streets of the capital strewn with muffling straw. In tune with his understated beginning, Sidney grew in contrast to his father to shun society and travel, while dedicating himself to his land, his inheritance. And this may have been the point at which the female side of the family first asserted itself.

Elizabeth Tringham (nee Boshier), Beth's mother, came of Anglo-Irish roots. Together with the auburn hair that her daughter would inherit, she possessed a delicacy of skin and complexion in contrast to the innate high colour of the Tringhams. What Elizabeth also possessed was a sensitivity, a deep appreciation of music and literature, wholly absent in her husband. As to how Elizabeth and Sidney met, how they embarked upon married life, how their first-born Simon came into the world, these are details that need not be related, for this is about Beth, just Beth.

Concerning Beth Tringham's early years, her life up to the age of 18 and the abrupt intrusion into her existence of Saul Dyneston, just one happening stands starkly out. Until she was 12 life stretched ahead lazily for the child Beth, untouched by the shadow of economic depression or rumours of war. In these early years midst the usual scares around measles and mumps, she was cherished by her parents, thoroughly spoiled and indulged by her brother Simon, the eight-year gap in their ages proving a boon rather than hindrance to their relationship.

One small incident when Beth was six, Simon 14, served to shape the bond between brother and sister. One evening when both Sidney and Elizabeth happened to be absent from the Manor House on parochial affairs, Beth was taking herself to bed at the top of the house. As usual she dragged over the little stool on which to stand to reach the light switch. She flicked the switch. At first nothing happened, so that she had to suppress her fear of the dark. But then a moment later a fierce fizzing came from the place where the light bulb was supposed to be. This was quickly followed by a lick of flame. In her panic Beth fell from her stool, crying out for Simon. Simon was by her side seemingly in seconds, taking in the scene at a glance. He flicked the wall switch up and immediately the flame appeared to collapse on itself. Simon scooped his sister into his arms and bore her down to his own bedroom. Beth was promised that someone would see to the faulty electrical connection, that if there was to be any delay he would see to it that his sister was given one of the old paraffin lamps to be going on with. Within minutes Beth was fast asleep in her brother's wide bed.

Simon Tringham of course was his father's heir to the Manor House, the Home Farm, 300 acres of fine stock-rearing lands, and family traditions that went back for as long as the first Tringham had been laid to rest in the graveyard of St Jude's. Simon was the boy who lived up to his parents' expectations in every way. Although there was no tradition of seafaring in the Tringham family, he enlisted in the sea scouts as early as possible, earning all of his badges, while leaving plenty of time to absorb the rudiments of the farming life. Aged 10, chosen to sing the opening verse of Once In Royal David's City, he completely captured the hearts of the packed congregation of St Jude's. The tingles that went down the spines of those worshippers, mothers and grandmothers especially, lingered and echoed in the memory for all of the 12 years before as a Sub-Lieutenant in a corvette Simon had been swept to his death in the freezing wastes of the North Atlantic. At the time the corvette had been escorting an eastbound convoy out of Halifax Nova Scotia.

Simon's death dislocated life for the Tringhams, setting them apart from each other on their own islands of grief. Simon's mother took to spending lonely hours slumped in a pew of St Jude's, a framed photograph of her son propped against the rail. Cooking and other household tasks were largely neglected so that Beth, young as she was, had to learn rapidly to stand in for her mother. The substitution was not achieved without inevitable hits and misses; yet no one seemed to care about that, while absorption in the repetitive demands of the day meant she was usually too tired to dwell on her brother's absence.

Of the three of them it was Simon's father whose inner being was most deeply disturbed, as a hanging rock finally submits to wind and weather, and falls. For Sidney Tringham had not only lost his son, he had also lost his heir. The result was a slow descent into chaos. The Home Farm it was that suffered the most. Milk returns got overlooked; farming machinery was allowed to go unserviced; stockmen came and went at frequent intervals; neighbouring land owners, personal friends among them, were met if at all with evasion, while tentative offers of help met only with stony indifference. A year or so after war's end and the Tringham estate, the nurture and wealth of generations tilted on the edge of bankruptcy.

Saul

Emerging at last from the snows and the floods of 1947, for the Weald there were tentative signs that six years of world war were settling back into history. Reserves of coal had run perilously low; rationing of clothing and staples of food seemed to be there for the duration; yet folk were beginning to realise it was no longer quite as necessary to guard against "loose lips" and "careless talk". Even old Lily Morris who kept the post office gradually tempered her bile towards "Prussans" and "Russans".

Beth Tringham acquired Molly, a piebald mare standing just over 14 hands unshod. Her ambition was to teach Molly to jump fences, even to compete at the county show if that ever got started again. So she began by rescuing a number of old hurdles from the back of a barn, and setting them out as an embryonic jump course around one of the fields that her father had allowed to go to grass.

Two more of Beth Tringham's teenage years drifted by in an undemanding dream. If she spent her waking hours in jodhpurs rather than dresses, if she carried the warm smell of horse flesh into the house, these were things of no consequence to her mother and father. Their daughter was a country girl, and there was time enough for hunt balls and all that malarkey. Then, quite out of the blue, everything changed.

* * *

Back-lit by the setting sun, Saul Dyneston materialised out of nowhere to lean his tall frame against a flagpole marking the boundary of the county show ground. He was dressed for the occasion. The double-breasted blue blazer was set off by a lavish purple cravat and jaunty panama hat, while a silk handkerchief peeped out of the breast pocket of the blazer. Shadowed by the panama, the face from a distance had a dark cast to it. Closer to it revealed a leathery sun burned look accentuating the white of the teeth and the wide curl of the mouth.

Saul Dyneston had no official business at the show that day, nor was he known to a single soul. That hardly bothered him. From the flagpole he marched in the direction of the grandstand, shooting stick cocked under arm, clipboard hoisted against his shoulder. Next to the members enclosure he erected his shooting stick on a lush patch of greenery, and settled to watch the final rounds of the jumping with the aid of binoculars that had last seen service in the hills south of Rome.

As Saul noted from the programme stapled to his clipboard, last to jump in the junior competition was Beth Tringham. As he scanned the arena he lifted an inch from his seat as, one by one, the fences were cleared. Then with the final post and rail approaching, the pony lost stride. With a visible effort girl and mount lifted over the obstruction. It was good, but not quite good enough. The topmost rail toppled and fell. Molly stumbled, recovered, plunged on towards the enclosure. Saul was on his feet in a second, racing to intercept pony and rider, as the crowd ringing the show ground broke into lively applause for the girl's near faultless round. At the gate of the enclosure he was just in time to come up on the girl and to grab the mare's bridle. Face glowing with the health of vigorous exertion, Beth slid down from the saddle. "Gosh! Thanks a lot. Haven'ta clue who you are, but you don't by any chance have a safety pin about your person, do you?"

Never slow on the uptake, Saul spotted the problem at once. One strap supporting the girl's jodhpurs had burst free of its seating so that her bottom half looked in sore danger of embarrassment. That final fence had done the damage. "Safety pin can't do, but how about this?" With a flourish he plucked the clip off the top of his clipboard to deftly secure the errant strap. "There you go, young lady, that'll at least see you as far as the changing room, yes?"

Giving a hitch to her jodhpurs Beth took up Molly's rein and started to head off. Over her shoulder she called back, "My saviour! I'll ask my father to stand you a beer in the bar."

"It was my pleasure. Name's Dyneston, by the way, Saul Dyneston. Also, if you don't mind me saying, looks as if young Molly's sweating up a bit. I should get a blanket on her sharpish if I was you."

* * *

Beth Tringham, or Beth Dyneston, has never said much about the man who abruptly emerged from obscurity to become her husband. Indeed the likelihood is she never knew much herself. So it follows it is unlikely that much can be offered by way of pedigree or family tree. All one can go on is rumour and innuendo.

In the four-ale bars of the district the first theory that did the rounds made Saul out to be nothing more nor less than a common horse dealer. This was supported by those who had seen him at horse fairs and around the weekly markets, and were able to swear that the newcomer knew his way around horse flesh. But then the idea that Dyneston might actually be a countryman was contradicted by the next rumour.

Drinking one evening in the nearby Nags Head, Dyneston, the smoker of flamboyant cigars, had discarded a match folder into the ashtray on the bar. Ever curious about foreign ways from up along and beyond the Weald, Kenny the barman had flicked open the folder to find that by naming a well known gentlemen's club the book of matches had originated on London's Pall Mall. The discovery soon bore fruit. A regular weekender in the lounge bar of the Nags, a Chancery barrister by profession, happened to have dining-in benefits at the club on Pall Mall. Returning home from the capital the King's Counsel was able to report he had managed to get a whiff of the cigar loving party. Of pedigree apparently there was no word; as for the old spondulicks, that was another matter. According to the handyman at Dyneston's club, "Party you be asking about, he's new to us. God knows who could have put him up for membership. Fond of flashing the old cash around, buying rounds of drinks and so on. Heard it said he was some sort of Quarter Master in the war, doing a handy business in jerry cans. Nothing to prove he was exactly wrong side of the tracks, but folks do chat that he returned from Italy a lot richer than when he arrived. Know what I mean?"

The big question is never likely to have an answer. Did "SD", as he liked to be known locally, have a notion to marry Beth Tringham before he set his sights on her father's farming estate, or was it the other way about? It is unlikely that Beth herself ever knew. Yet there were two things that she certainly did know. Beth knew this exotic creature from the outside world, this older man, was so much more exciting than any of the boys she came across at Young Farmers. And the second thing? She knew enough to realise if her father failed to act quickly, the farm, the whole estate including the Manor House would very soon be in the hands of the receiver with sale bills posted at every entrance to the rolling acres, the home she had known for as long as she could remember.

As Beth was not in the habit of drinking in the local hostelries, she was immune to the rumours about her fiancé. Apart from the occasional quizzical look from behind the counter of the village shop, as she thought about it much later, there was maybe just the one hint of what she might expect from marriage to Saul. The hint came from Bill Stancolm.

Bill Stancolm was local agent for the insurance company with whom the Tringham family had done business for a generation. To Beth he was a familiar face as, without fail, he would call at the Manor House each New Year to collect the premium for the next 12 months' cover, and to sit round the kitchen table to drink a cup of tea and chat awhile. But now, with father and mother Tringham receding into the background, Bill was yet keen to follow the tradition by doing business with Beth. And so it was that Beth sat him down in the kitchen, produced her purse, and counted out the money for a further 12 months' fire theft and accident insurance cover. In return the agent spread open his ledger, recited a summary of the cover for the Manor House, associated buildings and live and dead stock, before meticulously preparing his receipt of the premium monies. This done, he delved into his briefcase and produced a rather handsome looking plaque which he handed across the table to Beth. The plaque depicted in relief an exotic bird poised for flight from a nest of flames that bent back below the bird's wing. The bird of course was the mythical Phoenix. Bill explained the emblem was bound to adorn the front of Beth's ancestral home in the shape and character of a fire stone. Beth thanked the agent, adding that soon enough the Manor House would cease to be hers alone. For good measure she asked Bill if he had come across a Saul Dyneston. He offered neither a "yes" nor a "no," simply inclining his head on one side and thumbing his nose.

If Beth Tringham had dreamed of the traditional wedding in her beloved parish church, given away by her father, cheered by the villagers and garlanded with May blossom, she would have been severely disappointed. Instead of all that, SD whisked her to London on the pretext of introducing her to his *pied-a-terre* in Kensington and an evening at the ballet. That night they slept together for the first time. The following day, a Saturday, they were strolling together through Earls Court when Beth suddenly found she was standing in what Saul offhandedly referred to as a registry office. As SD scooped a couple of unsuspecting strangers off the pavement to act as witnesses, the truth finally dawned on his bride, the reason for the morning suit and the lavish buttonhole.

Emerging from the registry office in a daze, Beth was allowed to telephone her parents to convey a snatched and semi-coherent account of what had just happened to her before she was whisked down to Victoria and the Boat Train. The destination was northern Italy.

What Beth found she enjoyed most was the welcome, the civility with which they were greeted in most of the premier hotels, though the mosquitoes of Genoa proved rather less of a welcome. The bows of head waiters impressed, while the breakfast coffee and creamy gelatos at sundown in the lazy palazzos served to punctuate the daydream of her new life.

This perhaps was just as well as Mrs Dyneston quickly found that she and her husband struggled to seek out topics of conversation of mutual appeal. She knew somehow it must be her fault. At mealtimes she often found her tongue running away with itself. Having drawn a resounding blank with her love for the works of Jane Austen and other cherished memories of schooldays, she would fall back on her first love, that of eventing. Believing that the equine world was something they had in common, she babbled away about her plans to jump Molly The Second at senior level at the county shows that surely must be returning soon. In the process she kept forgetting that days only away the Tringham estate would no longer carry the ancient name.

During Beth's monologues her husband would tend to look not at his bride, rather more at his plate with snatched glances at the diary set down next the plate. He did however have the knack of nodding in the right places until often enough a waiter would sidle to their table bearing one or more telegrams on a silver tray. Beth was alert enough to know that telegrams meant business, so whenever this happened she cut short her rambles in midstream. Gradually it dawned on Beth she was on her honeymoon in name only. In reality she was being taken along on a business trip while matters of the bedroom seemed to alternate between the volcanic and the near comatose.

The truth finally hit Beth some days into the honeymoon. At her prompting Saul agreed they might hire a car and drive over the hills to Lake Como which Beth had heard was "As pretty as a picture postcard." They never reached the lake. Half way towards their destination her husband abruptly swung their hire car on to the forecourt of a petrol station and without a word of explanation made straight for the public telephone. For five minutes Beth sat stoically in the passenger seat with nothing but billboards to look at. Returning, Saul executed a gravel-churning u-turn, and they were racing back the way they had come. Soon enough a town came up, a town with a railway station. At the entrance to the station a stunted man beneath a battered straw hat loitered, something she took for a manifest of sorts tucked under his arm. Saul jumped from the car leaving the engine running while he greeted the stunted man in Italian and hustled him into the shade of a giant olive tree. Even had Beth possessed more than the odd word of Italian the two men were just too far away. All she picked up was the intermittent punctuation of a raised voice, her husband's voice. Back in the car, Saul at least had the grace to apologise. "My dear, I am so so sorry. You were looking forward to Como and I've spoilt it by having to look after a bit of business. We'll try again for the lakes tomorrow, yes?"

Leo, 1951

As the Forties tipped over into the Fifties and still no call-up to National Service arrived to trammel the undemanding progress of his career, Leo sometimes asked himself ruefully, "Am I in danger of ending up like Mr Chipps?"

The routine of Merelles was relentless. When not actually teaching, coaching in the cricket nets, or patrolling the junior dormitories, he yet felt that he was on duty most of the time. He had special responsibility in the Prep department which often meant the oversight of roller skating and conker competitions during breaks from lessons, and quite often the application of iodine with its telltale purple staining to bruised and bashed about young knees.

In the long evenings that followed school suppers of grizzled meats and stodgy coconut puddings, the residential masters could relax to a degree. Diversions for the boys amounted to simple pleasures most of which were wireless related. It was common when passing an open window to catch the vibrant signature tune of *Dick Barton Special Agent* or the urgent Coronation Scott music accompanying the latest criminal investigations of *Paul Temple*. Once hunkered down in bed many of the boys had cat's whisker wireless reception and were deterred from mischief being glued to Radio Luxembourg.

Alternate weekends brought a welcome break out from the college and its grounds. With rationing in full force there were no great excitements of a gastronomic kind, but luckily there was the cinema, the "flicks." Leo was usually collected by Will Piper in his Austin 7 and together they would drive into town to The Roxy. Pathé News was always worth watching as prelude to the latest film. One of their favourites just released was Alec Guinness in *The Lavender Hill Mob*. At the end of a showing they would stand for the National Anthem. This was partly out of a sense of propriety, but partly to avoid any entanglement with the growing ranks of local Teds with their brothel-creeper shoes and mildly threatening language of "square" and "cat" and "cool." It was a life that ambled along its routine way, that is, until something happened to puncture the easy rhythm.

It was Speech Day at Merelles and Leo was in charge of seating guests. At the top of his list was the aged admiral, a long-standing trustee of the college, whose turn it was to present the prizes. With 10 minutes to go before the start of the Headman's opening address, it was announced over the loud speaker that the admiral regretted he was indisposed and would not be able to attend this day. In his place and at very short notice, prizes were to be presented by "An up and coming Old Boy from the field of commerce and industry, Mr Jasper Earlham-Jones." And now here he was, EJ, sauntering towards the rostrum as if to the manor born.

Apart from one incident of a noisy throwing-up by an over excited Third Former, the annual ceremony passed off well. EJ in immaculate blazer and old school tie, performed his role with bravura verging on swagger, inserting the odd anecdote concerning his own time at the college. Ahead of the proceedings Leo was relieved to have only the briefest of contact with his bête noire; afterwards it was a different matter.

The two men bumped into one another outside the guests' bathrooms whence EJ was bound. "Ah! Church old man, I was planning to have words with you, would have tracked you down sooner or later. Today's shindig just makes it sooner. Let's chat in here." He put a shoulder to the swing door, half gesturing half pushing Leo into the bathrooms.

A lengthy relieving of the EJ bladder was followed by a dampening of the hair and serious communing with the mirror atop the hand basin. "See, it's like this, Church. I'm doing rather well these days, into property redevelopment, don't you know. Don't need to tell you, Master Fritz made a bit of a jolly mess of Old London Town, and it's up to people like me to, hmm, repair the damage, eh?"

Quite unsure where this was all leading, Leo backed to the far wall, folding arms, and doing his best to appear disengaged. "And this concerns me how?"

"Okay, so that's the thing. You'll be familiar with the saying, 'You can't build bricks without straw.' So of course for 'straw' read 'capital'. Of course my associates and I have the best of relations with the bankers, the very best; it's just that occasionally they tend to get just a little, hmm, formal."

"Meaning?"

"Meaning they are asking us for a guarantor, someone of impeccable character and background. So naturally I immediately thought of my old mentor and guide, in a word, of you, Church."

"But what I know about high finance can be written on the back of a postage stamp and …"

"Stop you right there old chap. That's not important. It's all about respectability, do you see?" He turned round from his studies in the mirror to face Leo across the room. "Financial nous, that doesn't matter a jot; what matters is, hmm, dependability. So, what do you say, are you okay to stamp your monica on a couple of forms? They're right here in my case."

At that moment the door of the bathrooms swung open to admit a roistering bevy of fathers and uncles relaxed by the liquid element of their luncheon. Leo saw his chance to escape and took it without a moment of hesitation. Briskly he headed for his turret room atop the tower.

Leo was half way up the first flight of stairs when he was called back by the Headman. "I say Church!" The Headman looked flustered. "Seems I am about to be cornered by the parents of young Rhodes Minor, something to do with an alleged allergy to our semolina puddings. Would you mind awfully escorting our guest of honour to his motor car and waving him off with my grateful thanks for stepping into the breach at short notice?" Seeing that he had no choice in the matter Leo turned about and went in search of EJ.

The guest of honour was easily located, holding court to an admiring circle of Sixth Formers on the terrace. Leo edged into the circle, managing to get a word in to explain his mission. Flourishing court bows all around, EJ tucked her briefcase under arm and headed for the car park, Leo trailing behind him. Reaching his car, a silver coloured 1930's Bentley, EJ turned about, conjuring a sheaf of paperwork out of his case while unclipping a Parker pen from his breast pocket. "Thought you would enter the lists, come up to the mark, old chap."

Leo edged his back against the fender of the Bentley, shoving hands in pockets, giving his best imitation of nonchalance. "Why should I do anything for you, Earlham-Jones? If I recall, we parted not exactly on the best of terms."

EJ stood side on to Leo, one arm casually resting across the roof of the Bentley. "Too right old sport. Could have got me the sack, rusticated at least.

Of course you weren't to know the pater had just signed a fat cheque to pay for restoration of the squash courts, eh?"

"No I didn't know that, but …"

"Now see here, Church. Back in the day I seem to remember you could be a bit, hmm, handy yourself, eh?"

To his embarrassment Leo felt blood surge into his neck. "What on earth are you talking about?"

"Ah well, this is the thing. A year or two back we, I happened to bump into young Williams. We were strap-hanging together on the Bakerloo line. Got talking as old Merellesians do. Your name just had to come up. Seems you had a bit of a fancy for our Spider, or should I say "spoider" back in the day. Liked to get him on his own in the detention room, did you not?"

Leo jack-knifed off the Bentley's fender, hands on hips, fixing his tormentor with a stare. "That is total rubbish. Of course I remember Williams, always on about spiders and flies, but I'm sorry, his imagination has clearly taken over his pathetic mind, and you ought to know better than to trot this rubbish out."

"Only trouble is – trouble for you I mean, young Williams might just be tempted to make a case out of it. Turns out he's started out on a career as a clerk with one of the capital's top law firms, so statements and affidavits are meat and drink for our Spider. I'm quite sure the last thing you would want is that he drops a note to Merelles' chairman of trustees, eh? Could be the end of a beautiful career for you."

With horrible deliberation the cap was removed from the Parker pen.

Beth and Saul

Back home life for Beth settled to a pattern. She was not sorry. She had still to reach her twentieth birthday, yet the headlong progress of courtship, marriage and honeymoon had taken her breath away. What she had managed to teach herself about the running of a household during the difficult years following Simon's death came to her aid. One big exception was wines, their provenance, their vintages, their harmonious relation to different dishes. Her total ignorance when it came to the ordering, the storage, the serving of wine was soon a point of friction.

While Beth took hesitant steps to grow into being a wife, her husband carried on as if his young bride was little more than a pebble in his stream. Most weeks he seemed content to leave Beth in the country while he presumably went about business in London, hanging his hat in Kensington. With rare exceptions he returned to the Manor House for the weekend.

Surprisingly perhaps, the weeks failed to pall, for she made of them a routine of her own. Twice weekly she accompanied her mother to early Holy Communion at St Jude's, returning with her to her parents' annex home to drink coffee and discuss the racing columns of the newspapers with her father. Beth felt no deep connection to the mysteries of the bread and the wine; but the racing pages never failed to spark an interest. She felt profoundly for each of her parents, her feelings compounded of loyalty and a sense of embarrassment at the fall in their circumstances aggravated by her husband's behaviour.

During school holidays and on Tuesdays and Thursdays in the evenings in term time she conducted structured classes for the children of the district to impart the rudiments of riding, how to handle stirrups, saddle and bit, how to seat their mount and how to trot the pony. She quickly found her classes were so popular, the parents so enthusiastic and full of praise for her efforts and expertise, that she found it necessary to take on a young girl as assistant. Good too was the money. The income was not of a life changing order, yet it served to spark a modest sense of independence.

If between times Beth found herself at a loose end, her favourite recourse was to Far Goose Spinney on the margin of the Manor lands. The reason it was Beth's favourite was its connection with Simon. Times in years gone by brother and sister would repair hand in hand to the spinney, just to be on their own. Set down on a ridge overlooking the Pilgrims Way, the spinney for Beth was an enchanted fastness. From beneath his blond fringe Simon would stare out across the weald, helping his sister to count the oast houses dotted over the landscape, while dreamingly reciting the plans he wanted to present to their father for the expansion of the farming estate. While Simon talked, Beth listened, dreaming along with her brother. Now there was no Simon, yet her visits to the spinney somehow brought him back to her with a comforting warmth.

Friday evening would see Beth start out for the station in pony and trap, returning often not just with SD but with one or more hangers-on. These hangers-on seldom endeared themselves to Beth. To a man they proved to be hard drinkers and never too careful about the discarding of cigar buts. Beth's parents now much reduced in their quality of living and shut away in the annex, at first tried saying something about their son-in-law's guests but soon backed off in the face of stony indifference from their son-in-law. Beth herself said nothing, did nothing.

That is, she did nothing until one day a confrontation forced her hand.

Of the weekend visitors most of whom ignored their nominal hostess, there was one who seemed determined to catch her eye and draw her into conversation. This was a man name of Dawson. Sallow of face, sporting ferocious eyebrows, Dawson as he introduced himself to Beth, was a jobber. As the term meant nothing to the young wife, Dawson embarked upon a lengthy and detailed explanation of London's stock markets. But as Beth struggled to hide her boredom, Dawson abruptly changed tack.

At the time chatelaine and guest were face to face on the narrow path that led back from the orchard. Beth was carrying a heavy pannier of plums so that both of her hands were occupied. Dawson made no move to get out of the way; instead he fixed his friend's wife with a come-hither look while reaching a manicured hand out to loop an auburn curl behind her ear. "This is well met, young lady. Why don't we ditch those plums of yours and continue our chat down there in your ever so comfortable summerhouse. What do you say?" This with a gentle tweak of the curl.

Blushing hotly, Beth conjured a side step, leaving Dawson flat-footed in the middle of the path. Over her shoulder she shot back that if she did not get on pretty quick and do something about that evening's meal she was afraid they would all go hungry.

In bed that night, haltingly Beth recited the embarrassing incident on the path from the orchard. SD was late to their bed, his mood elated by many a toast with his guests. Instead of concern what he threw back at his wife was convulsions of mirth. When the mirth came to an end, he lay back in the bed, tilted his wine-red face in his wife's direction, sighed extravagantly and said, "Dear Girl, you should know by now, you ought to be nice to my friends, yes?" Naive though she knew herself to be, Beth did not fail to intuit exactly what was meant by "nice."

* * *

By degrees Beth attuned herself to the waves of married life, gradually coming to the realisation that nothing was going to change. Keeping house to the wayward demands of her husband got no easier. Holding on to the services of the village girls was a problem. Worldly enough, for the most part they were able to give and take when it came to the pinching of bottoms, though leaving tips proved stingy and rare. Yet there were compensations. For one thing, Saul himself was not mean with money, so that the occasional new dress was encouraged, even applauded, rather than begrudged. For another thing, there seemed to be no urgency about her becoming pregnant, something that Beth felt obscurely unsettled about.

Then one day, it was a Saturday towards the end of March, everything changed in the course of a few frantic minutes. Beth was up and doing early, enticed by the savour of spring carried on the westerly breeze. A good long outing on Molly was exactly what both she and the pony needed. As it happened, this fitted with Saul's own plans for the day. He had a party coming from London, but he would not need Beth to play hostess as, "Dare say we'll likely dine out."

Beth stayed long enough to spruce the cushions and set out trays of glasses and drinks, then changed into her jodhpurs. As she exited the house she was in time to greet her husband's guests, a party of six or seven, which included two women sailing confidently forward beneath picture hats.

In the stables a shock awaited Beth. Usually Molly would be waiting, head thrust forward, ears pricked. This day Beth found her slumped down on her hay, apathetic to the world.

Inside the mare's stall Beth bent to talk to her old friend. Molly responded, clambering shakily to her feet. Yet something was wrong. Mentally Beth ticked off possible causes. Of injury there was no sign. Perhaps there was something amiss with her feed. That too was most unlikely as Beth mixed the feed herself. Hands on hips she was puzzling what on earth to do when a shadow fell across the upper half of the stable door.

Saul had that look on his face that Beth recognised as his "don't get near me" look. Bustling into the stall he took one glance at the mare before reaching for the strap that Beth sometimes used as a leading rein when tutoring the children in their classes. His first blow caught Molly across her belly; the second blow bisected her eyes. Rooted to the spot, Beth dimly understood that Molly was being chastised for nothing more venal than laziness. She also understood that somehow she herself was being punished for not being gone.

Without a word, Saul threw away the strap and stalked from the stall without the least glance in his wife's direction. From over at the house came the plaintive strains of Armstrong's trumpet and West End Blues, a soundtrack to misery that would haunt Beth through the years to come.

Leo, 1952

It was the first day of term at Merelles Academy, and the borders of the grand drive blazed with colour. Boys tumbled out of parental vehicles flourishing brand new Alec Bedser bats soon to be elaborately distressed, while junior masters strutted about, clipboards readied.

Leo Church kept his distance. Long gone were the days when he felt it necessary to ingratiate himself with either boys or parents. Instead he made his way to his pigeonhole to see what post might have accumulated during the Easter holidays.

Apart from professional magazines there were just two items. One was a brown envelope bearing a central London postmark; the other was a white envelope with the postmark nearest to his mother's home. Both were addressed to him in type and had a bit of an official look to them. Backing away to the bench outside the porter's lodge, Leo opted to open the white envelope first, a prick of conscience warning him this was something to do with Jeanie. The reason for the conscience lay in the fact that he had seen his mother only the once, and then fleetingly right back at the start of the holidays, the rest of which had been taken up with his walking tour in the Cotswolds quickly followed by a week in London with his old friend Will Piper, who had left Merelles the year before for a senior master post at Westminster School.

Despite his premonition Leo was startled by what he read while sinking himself down to the bench. Easing his glasses upwards, he nervously rubbed at his nose while rereading the letter from his family's medical practice. The letter was signed personally by Daniel Owens, the senior partner and his mother's own doctor which convinced Leo that it bore the stamp of truth.

In Owens' crisp no-nonsense style the letter informed Leo that with his patient's consent, Owens was writing to advise Leo as Mrs Church's next of kin that he, Daniel Owens MD, had concerns regarding his mother's state of health. It appeared that the good doctor had seen Jeanie three times since

Christmas and on each occasion had noticed a slight but progressive deterioration in his patient's cognitive function. The letter fell short of clinical detail let alone prognosis; yet the passing reference to memory loss clearly pointed Leo in the direction of dementia, despite the doctor's reference to "early stages."

Up and down the corridor leading away from the porter's lodge hallooed greetings echoed, punctuated by bursts of hilarity. Leo was barely aware of any of it. Doctor Owens finished his letter by assuring Leo that there was no immediate cause for panic, but that a filial visit might not go amiss while, more vaguely, that planning for the future "might well be necessary." Leo re-folded the letter and slowly tucked it back inside its envelope. He wiped his glasses and stared unseeing at the print of The Fighting Temeraire that faced him across the lobby. Another minute and he was back to his feet. He marched across Great Hall, crossed over the terrace, and strode the 300 yards to the wrought iron gates that marked the boundary of Merelles. Over the boundary and seemingly in his absence a little colony of prefabs* had materialised as fast as a rash of spring mushrooms. Women were pegging washing out to dry; somewhere a wireless crooned. With a renewed flush of guilt he knew he had to do something about his mother. He reached into his pocket, intent on re-reading Dr Owens' letter. Instead his hand came out with the brown envelope which now he opened with an impatient tear.

Leo read the enclosed letter three times before the contents sank in. The letter on official notepaper was from the bank, Earlham-Jones' bank, more precisely from the directors of that bank. In a few terse paragraphs it informed Leo that their customer's account had recently gone into "unauthorised overdraft" and that in consequence no further cheques drawn on the account would be honoured by the bank. It was however open to Mr Church as Guarantor of the account to remedy "the regrettable situation" by immediately remitting the sum of £1,937.22 (one thousand nine hundred and thirty-seven pounds and twenty-two pence) in order to place the account back in credit. The directors therefore hoped that they would hear from Mr Church at his most urgent convenience. They closed by assuring him that they remained his "Obedient Servants."

Leo found that the hand holding the letter was shaking. To get rid of the

---

* Bombing had reduced Britain's housing stock by some 74,000 units. The loss had to be remedied by the fastest and most economical means. The answer was prefabrication, hence the replacement dwellings were nicknamed "Prefabs."

shaking and to relieve his feelings, he promptly tore the letter into many very small pieces, allowing the confetti to sail away on the breeze.

Back in school Leo made a beeline for the Headman's office, intent on showing his employer Dr Owens's letter and requesting leave of absence on compassionate grounds. The Headman was not in his office. His secretary explained that he was touring the school with a party of prospective parents, and was not expected back for some time. Did Mr Church wish to leave a message? Leo only thought for a moment. He fished out the doctor's letter, dashed down a brief note on the envelope, and asked the secretary if she would kindly "Give this to the Old Man as soon as you see him, please."

Leo spent three days with his mother. He was relieved to find that Jeanie appeared to be in good spirits and more relaxed than he had known her of late. She was open about her visits to her doctor, though sorry that Leo had needed to break away from the new term "To see your old mother." Once or twice he caught Jeanie struggling to find her words or recall a family or a neighbour's name; but that apart, she seemed to be perfectly well. So Leo returned to Merelles on the third day of his unscheduled absence.

The first time that Leo and the Headman crossed in the corridor Leo was treated to a black look though no word passed between the men at that time. Leo buckled down to his work and even volunteered to do an extra coaching session for the Colts in the cricket nets. Then as May turned into June a second letter arrived from Earlham-Jones' bank. Leo read that the directors were "extremely disappointed" not to have heard by way of reply to their earlier correspondence. Furthermore they had to inform Mr Church that they were considering formal proceedings to invoke his guarantee, proceedings that would "inevitably incur legal costs and possible distraint[*] against personal property."

As Leo's "personal property" amounted to some £30 plus a couple of first edition folios, he decided to ignore the letter. His only thought was, "Strange I've never heard anything from EJ himself. Haven't exactly been looking for a dividend by way of acknowledging the guarantor thing; but why hasn't there been a letter, a telephone call, even a visit in person to turn the screw?" With the end of term in sight, Leo was to discover that his old nemesis had not been idle after all.

---

[*] The legal remedy known as "Distraint" refers to the seizing of personal property in satisfaction or part-satisfaction of a debt.

It was the last morning of term, the last day of the academic year, and Leo was sat in a corner of the library, making notes for next year's timetable. Breathless and perspiring, diminutive Bincks Minor bustled up to Leo. "Sir, Sir, the headmaster convoys his gre-gre-greetings and please can he see you in his study straightaway."

As usual, Leo affected to ignore the boy's stammer while gently correcting Bincks' vocabulary. "Thank you Bincks, but I think you mean to tell me that our reverend headmaster wishes to convey his greetings. Go back and say that I am on my way. And Bincks, don't run, eh?"

As well as his best Sunday suit, the headmaster was sporting his dog collar, no doubt to impress upon parents that as well as Merelles Headman he was also a Man of God. Leo was bidden to take a seat across the desk from his employer who sat huffing and polishing at his spectacles for some moments before clearing his throat and addressing the wall behind Leo's head. "Well now Church, I have to tell you that I have received a rather disturbing letter from an old Merellesian which I am afraid relates to yourself."

The Headman paused, perhaps hoping that Leo would say something to ease his flow. Leo remained silent. "So, yes, the correspondence was from young Earlham-Jones late of this parish, and it seems that he accuses you of, improper behaviour with one of our juniors."

"The name of the junior?"

"Williams."

"And when is this supposed to have taken place?"

"As to that, well, Earlham-Jones doesn't exactly say. Must have been a year or two ago, I suppose." The last few words were mumbled into the Headman's beard.

Leo jerked forward. "Head Master, you need to know that Earlham-Jones and I parted on bad terms after I had to reprimand him for, well, mishandling one of our laundry girls, an unsavoury episode which I am sure you were informed about. Ever since then he has been trying to blackmail me with the false accusation to which you refer."

"Don't know about that, Church. But what I do know is that the merest whiff of scandal is not to be borne. Trustees just won't wear it, do you see?"

A long silence gathered in the close air of the study. Finally the Headman spoke again. "So it comes down to this. I am sorry, Church, but we really have no option but to let you go." He fished in his desk and produced a buff envelope which he spun across the desk. "In writing this testimonial I decided to overlook your unscheduled absence from the school at the start of term. Instead I have emphasised your qualities as a teacher, oh and your contribution to Merelles cricket." Getting to his feet, "And now I have a governors' meeting to attend."

After a short duty visit to Jeanie, Leo sought refuge with Will in Will's Knightsbridge flat, and began the business of combing advertisements for teaching posts. As he had to admit, that testimonial had been cleverly worded so that Leo had no qualms about producing it to a potential employer. While one day he was kicking his heels around town, it suddenly occurred to Leo he had a visit pride demanded he make.

The bank turned out to be right on Leo's doorstep. Dressed in his best suit and tie, and flourishing a briefcase, he managed to fool the teller in the banking hall into believing he had an appointment with the manager. Admitted to the inner sanctum, he introduced himself by thrusting his birth certificate across the desk by way of identification. While the manager scrutinised the document, Leo glanced around the office, telling himself that the mustard-coloured brocade wallpaper did not really make him feel sick.

Asked what the manager could do for him, Leo wasted no time at all by requesting to see the deed of guarantee signed back in the day of the heat of the school's car park. The manager dissembled, but having to acknowledge that his visitor was a party to the document in question, finally went to a cabinet and duly produced the guarantee. A mere glance was enough for Leo to recognise his signature, but also to take in that despite the printed direction, the signature had never been witnessed. This he drew to the attention of the manager before calmly pouching the document and sliding it into his briefcase. The manager's hand was still stretched across the desk awaiting the return of the paperwork as Leo turned to go. Should he dread the unknown consequences of his instinctive action? Leo decided that he did not care.

September tipped over into October. Leo's mood was as black as the fog that pressed down into the streets of West London. There were no replies to any of his many applications for employment. Will of course was the best of company while not at school; but Leo was beginning to worry that he was outstaying his welcome.

Finally a letter. The letter came from a crammer establishment in Liverpool. Leo understood that they wanted him. More than that, they wanted him urgently as a member of their staff had just died. So could Mr Church please come for interview as soon as possible. Travel and overnight expenses would be reimbursed in full.

On the day fixed for the interview Leo was up and doing while it was still dark outside. Calling over his shoulder to his friend in response to Will's "Hope it goes well for you old chap," Leo shouted back that he might have the luck to catch the eight o'clock express from Euston.

PART II

Beth Travelling

When Beth Tringham had slipped from the neck of her first pony at the age of nine, her father, after checking her over for any signs of injury, had sternly advised his daughter, "What do you do after you've had a fall? You get right back on the horse," advice that Beth had benefited from over the years. Now, as the pullman eased away from Waterloo's Platform Four, she was not at all sure that what applied to horses applied equally to trains.

Beth was on her way to Bournemouth to see her parents for the first time since the disaster of October 8th. A year earlier her mother and father, Sidney and Elizabeth, had left the Manor House and the hateful sight of their son-in-law, to eke out their slender means in a guest house on Bournemouth's Shelley Road, where Beth's mother had found a home of sorts with the local Anglican church, while her father had tracked down partners for regular hands of whist.

As a consequence of separating from her husband, Beth's day to day circumstances had changed. To begin with, and while enrolling in a crash course for aspiring secretaries, she had camped out in the Kensington flat while enduring the reminders, not least the smell of Saul Dyneston and his foul cigars that ambushed Beth around every corner. Her feelings about marriage, about her marriage, swung violently back and forth. There were days when she stared at the mirror and blamed herself for the abject failure of her marriage. She was a prude; she was unworldly; she had made no effort to understand her sophisticated husband. Within the hour another glance in the mirror revealed flaming cheeks and resolute line of mouth. The incident with Molly had finally opened her eyes. Saul Dyneston was only interested in exploiting others; cruelty was bred in his bones; he was what her Aunt Evelyn would have called, "an out and out bastard." There had been no contact between husband and wife for weeks. Beth assumed

Saul was relishing having the run of the Manor House to entertain his freeloading friends and associates. He was welcome to it. She no longer had to clear up after them; no longer had to dodge the pinches aimed at her bottom. Meantime Beth had had not one but two strokes of luck. At the conclusion of her secretarial course she had landed a job in the Royal Courts of Justice, that warren of stone corridors and wood-panelled rooms for so long a landmark on London's Strand. Secondly, thanks to Hannah, a friend from her school days, she had found a cramped but cheap attic flat behind Flood Street Chelsea. All of that was before the crash.

Beth's recovery from the trauma of the rail crash was a much slower, more complex matter. The facts in all their brutal simplicity haunted her night and day. The driver of the express that had started its journey in Perth had missed a danger signal in the fog and had ploughed into the back of a local service being held at a platform of Harrow and Wealdstone station. Moments later the double-headed Liverpool train, her train, travelling at 60 miles per hour, had charged into the wreckage of the first collision. As Beth had learned from the following day's newspapers, no less than 112 travellers had been killed and over 300 injured. Those deaths included seven from the Liverpool train whose kitchen car had been destroyed along with the 11 coaches forward of it. Casualties it was reported could have been even more catastrophic but for two things. A quick thinking railwayman had disconnected the electric current to the tracks, while a medical unit from American forces based at South Ruislip had reached the scene within minutes. One member of this unit, an African-American nurse, by name, Lieutenant Abbie Sweetwine had saved lives and earned the sobriquet "The Angel Of Platform 6." The "Angel" and her fellow medics, it was reported, had employed trauma techniques learned in the world war, while Abbie Sweetwine herself had improvised with the aid of a lipstick to mark the foreheads of those casualties receiving morphine shots at the scene of the crash, so as to avoid the possibility of later overdosing of the analgesic.

One death in particular had haunted Beth ever since reading about the man who had rushed to the scene bearing specialist metal cutting equipment. This man would have acted as he did, come what may; yet he knew that his daughter was likely to have taken the commuter train into Euston. Hours of frantic toil later, his daughter's body had been found deep in the wreckage of the train.

Over the weeks and indeed the years to come, mountains of print would pile up in the form of reports and formal recommendations; but those were the bare facts which would never change, never reprieve a single life lost.

Her own experience was and remained far less clear in Beth's mind and there were times when she counted that as some sort of blessing. Her removal from the wreckage of the rearmost coach was a blur. She could remember arriving in a hospital, and marvelling at the speed that had taken her there. In the hospital she must have been treated for numerous cuts and bruises as miles of bandaging and stink of antiseptic testified. She was kept there for a day and a night – or was it two days and two nights – on account of concussion. She was then brought a telephone on a trolley, and invited by one of the incredibly caring nurses to phone family or friends. Beth did not feel ready to contact anyone apart from the school friend who had put the Chelsea flat her way. Hannah was at the hospital in little more than an hour. Beth was provided with a stock of pain killers and discharged. She fell into the comfort of her own bed. All that she wanted to do was sleep; but sometime in the dark watches of the night her recovering mind was hit by the jagged image of a young man with a shard of glass protruding from his eye.

Now Beth's Bournemouth train was picking up speed. Round about Clapham Junction sets of points rattled and juddered through her spine. She feared she was about to have some sort of panic attack with no one in her compartment to help her. At the same moment the door of the compartment crashed back to admit a man who had to stoop to cross the threshold from the corridor. "Do you mind I join you, *madame?*"

"Oh please do." Beth looked up to see a rangy individual, thin as a lath, clean-shaven, and with grey eyes that at once caught and held her attention.

The man swung a briefcase to the rack before sitting down precisely opposite to Beth. "I do thank you. Do you allow me to introduce myself? When in France I am Jean-Paul, but mostly I am in England since 1940, and here I am simply Paul. But excuse me, you do look most pale in your face. Are you all right?" The voice was baritone with undertones of authority, yet the question was put with feeling.

"Oh yes, thank you, I'm all right, now," was Beth's halting reply as she surreptitiously pinched a cheek to bring colour to her face.

But her companion was quick to catch the slight pause before the "now." Half rising, "I have a little brandy. Perhaps …"

"No really. I'm fine. I'll be fine. But thank you." This with her best effort at a smile.

Paul was sat down again. "Naturally, it is not my business, but perhaps you have had a shock, no?

"It's just that, hmm, that I was recently in a, a rather bad accident, a quite serious train smash actually, so this is me getting back on the horse, if you see what I mean. But I'd love it if you talk, tell me about yourself. It'll take my mind off trains."

"Of course, well I too am on my way to Bournemouth. I am required to see someone in Bournemouth, someone who distinguished herself in the last war. I regret, I am not free to say more about that even now, but you may know that I am attached to France's embassy and, well, seem to have made my home now in this lovely England of yours. I do not think it is a secret to tell you that I first landed in England with the General for whom I worked until he returned to La Belle France to march up the aisle of Notre Dame de Paris."

Just then the door of the compartment crashed back and there was the collector of tickets, hand held out. "Thank you sir, thank you madam. Bournemouth Central no change." Making use of the diversion Beth pinched her other cheek and sneaked a furtive look at the mirror opposite. What she saw was an oval face framed by a rush of auburn hair reaching to her shoulder. The nose was perhaps a fraction too large, but the greeny-brown eyes remained full of life. She was thankful to see that her cheeks now had colour. The ticket collector slammed shut the door and bustled on to the next compartment.

"I am sorry that you have had this very bad experience. May I guess that you were on the train out of Euston, and does it help you to talk about it, or maybe not?"

For a moment Beth gazed out of the window as the train flashed through a small station. Then haltingly she started on the story. Paul made no attempt to interrupt, but kept his eyes on the storyteller the whole time. Eventually Beth ran out of words which was when her companion spoke for the first time. "So dear lady, you speak from the heart, and you tell me things that interest me greatly. You tell me it is your habit to take this train each Saturday, yet for reasons that are unimportant this time you had to travel on a Wednesday. You tell me that given the chance you would have made for the kitchen car, but because you were in danger of missing the train you made a grab for the last carriage. I wonder, do you feel you are the victim of coincidence or the beneficiary – is that the right word? – of coincidence?" A small gesture of the hand. "But perhaps we skip the metaphysics, yes?" *

With a smile, "Oh yes, let's skip the metaphysics."

"But then there is something else that interests me. Thankfully it seems you were not badly wounded, certainly not in your body. But what of the young man who was with you in your compartment? Of course you were concerned about him and his fate. Indeed you tell me that in the days following the disaster you contacted several hospitals hoping that you might trace the man and hopefully learn of his recovery. You had no luck, yet I do not hear you say that you tried the famous hospital which I think is called Moorfields, which I think is the specialist for the treatment of the eyes. This hospital, it is in the east end of London, is it not? You have the determination I think to find this man; but you must realise that having found him the outcome will be uncertain. With luck all will be well. You may exchange your addresses and send each other a card each Noël. Chance though may reveal a damaged soul. You may be haunted for the rest of your life by your failure – as you might see it – to come to his aid in the wreckage of the train, no?"

Despite herself, Beth felt her blood rising to a blush. "I think you must be able to read my thoughts. Makes me think of my work. I work as a stenographer at the Old Bailey. The lawyers when they're questioning the witnesses like to pose their questions, their cross-examinations as if somehow they inhabit the minds of those witnesses, and already know the answers to their questions. It's what my Aunt Evelyn would call, 'A bit spooky.' Anyway, you're not wrong – about how I feel, I mean."

A long silence while Beth stared out of one window, the Frenchman out

---

* The Danish philosopher Kirkegard was first to socialise the concept of Existentialism across the continent of Europe; but it was the writings of French-Algerian Albert Camus who later popularised the concept in Britain before and after the author's death in a car crash in 1960. The arrival of Existentialism in Britain was largely brought about through the publication of three works of fiction, *The Fall*, *The Plague*, and *The Outsider*, the last named becoming a regular choice for advanced level students.

of the other. Finally Paul turned back to his companion. "I would like to ask you a question, but please, you do not have to answer my question if it is too, hmm, personal."

Beth met the blue eyes. "Oh, I don't mind. What do you want to ask me?"

"I cannot help to notice that you wear a ring which I think is a wedding ring. Is your husband perhaps absent to do with his business, or was he too involved in the smash of the train?"

"My husband? No no, he wasn't anywhere near Euston on the 8th of October. As for business, well you could say he's always doing some sort of business or other." Head bowed, she muttered the last bit of her reply. "We no longer live together, we're no longer together."

"And yet you still wear the ring?"

"I suppose I'm no different from a lot of women, women whose husbands were killed in the war, for example. We continue to wear our rings as some sort of protection. Either that or we can't get the bloody things off!" ending with a self-conscious burst of a laugh.

"Do you want to talk about your husband?"

"No, I don't think I do, thank you."

"I see you looking at my hand," tapping his left hand. "No, I am not married except to my work. Besides, I do not think any woman would have me and the chaos of my flat. But happily I expect a visit from my young niece Cecilie, who will be coming to this country to improve her English – and to sort me out, if that is the right expression."

Once again they fell silent. Paul reached down his briefcase and extracted a bundle of papers which occupied him in fierce concentration until the brakes of the train engaged with a jolt.

"I think we might be coming into our destination. I am pleased we have had our conversation. I would like to offer you my card because I am curious about the young man in the train, and would like to hear news of him if you do me the favour of writing me or telephoning me?"

Beth took the card, glancing at the embossed script. Gathering suitcase and handbag to her, Beth looked back from the door of the compartment. "I'll do that. And thank you."

Hilly

For Beth, work was demanding, almost all-absorbing. Back home from The Strand and hidden away in the mews flat, she found she had little energy to do anything of an evening other than heat a pan of soup and catch the Nine o'clock news on the wireless Home Service. Her weekends were a little more liberating. Unless it was raining cats and dogs, she chose often to ramble through the royal parks or to window-shop in the Tottenham Court Road. As she walked, one subject preoccupied Beth, and that was the advice of the Frenchman Paul, following the serendipity of their meeting. And so it was that, early in the New Year, she acted.

While not that far from the centre of the capital, Caton Street lay further east than Beth had previously ventured. Beth's first impression was that the hospital looked a bit sorry for itself with a number of its windows boarded up. This impression was underlined by the lingering shadow of war, the undisturbed presence of more than one bomb site in the general vicinity. A lowering layer of fog or smog did nothing to enhance the beauty of the area.

As it was a Saturday, Beth vaguely imagined the hospital would be more relaxed and therefore more receptive to her quest, although she had no notion why she thought this. In any case she was wrong. Moorfields foyer bustled with people, some in civvies, rather more in starchy white uniform, all scuttling determinedly head down. Beth tried to catch the attention of one or two of the white coats, but was brushed aside each time. Her confidence began to fail and she retreated to a waiting area away from the concourse. There she slumped onto a chair next to a stricken looking mother, her arm around the narrow shoulders of a boy wearing a large eye patch. Beth closed her eyes, sank her head into her chest.

Ten minutes dragged by. Then came a voice in Beth's ear and she turned to face a motherly looking woman wearing a neat white badge with the hospital's logo above the inscription "Registered Volunteer." "You're looking as if you've lost a pound and found a penny. What's up Dear?"

Beth stared up at the woman for several moments. "Oh, it's just that I've come here hoping to get news of someone, someone who was injured in the Harrow crash."

"And the name of this someone?"

"Well that's the problem. I don't know his name, but he was in the same compartment as me. His glasses were smashed, and he had something in his eye."

"Wait on there, my love, and I'll ask for you. My name's Ivy, by the way."

It was a quarter of an hour before Ivy returned. "Ok Dear, so I might have narrowed it down for you. Seems there were five casualties from that awful business who were brought here for treatment."

"Oh gosh, as many as that?"

"As many as that. But the good news for you, only one of those five was male."

Blood flooded back into Beth's face, a little more animation into her eyes. "This man, is he still a patient here?"

"I'm told he is not. I'm told he was discharged before Christmas." Ivy sat down next to Beth, and took one of her hands in her own. "You'll be wanting to contact this gentleman no doubt, find out how he's getting along. Am I right?"

"Yes."

"So, the hospital won't give you out his address; but I tell you what, if you'd like to write me out your own address along with the reason for wanting to be in touch, I'll make sure it will be forwarded on to Mr Mystery Man." And with this, Ivy unpinned her badge and handed it to Beth, plain side uppermost, together with a stub of pencil.

Returning home on the bus, Beth fixed her mind on the strong mug of Indian tea that would help her to wrap her mind around the possibilities that her morning's adventure might yet uncover. So focused as she was on that possibility, there was no way that she was prepared for the shock that waited for her and would drive all thoughts of the crash and the young man out of her mind. For in the act of knocking at her front door, the telegraph boy stood, buff envelope in hand.

* * *

Beth instructed her taxi to put her down a mile short of the Manor House. Speeding her down to the Weald, her train had been packed to the aisles with holiday-makers so that she had found it impossible to focus her mind on her husband's frantic message. From the terse wording of the telegram she gathered that Saul had something most important and most urgent to discuss with her. He would have come to London to see her in Chelsea, but was laid up following an accident.

As Beth turned into Dogrose Lane with the white gables of her old home peeping at her over the crest, it registered with her that the day was the very best of early summer. The hedgerows danced and chorused with the industry of nesting birds, song thrushes and, yes, the occasional yellow hammer. Dotted along the verge a late flowering of marsh marigolds shone up at her. Away to one side of the path the drone of a tractor harrowing Long Acre brought back memories all but buried by the years of urban dwelling. The prospect of once more confronting Saul Dyneston cut across the idyll like a knife. She had no idea what could be so very urgent. Since they had gone their separate ways, there had been virtually no contact between husband and wife; nor had a penny of maintenance been forthcoming. And what was this about an accident? The Saul she knew was not the sort to have accidents. Of course he'd always gone in for fast driving. This Beth knew only too well. There had been times, she remembered now, when with the roof wide open he had driven them so fast to some party or other that her hair had been a total mess on arrival. Knowing how proud she was of her auburn tresses, had he done this on purpose? Recalling this while turning into the drive to the Manor House, Beth dodged behind a tree to check her appearance in her compact mirror. As she placed a foot on the first of the steps leading to the front door of the house, the last thing she noticed was a line of cumulus cloud massing, bruising the skyline some way off to the west.

The door stood open. Saul Dyneston was waiting for her in the conservatory. He lounged back on the old Persian recliner, drink in hand, right leg propped up on an occasional table. "Ah, so you got my telegram. Come in, come and sit down, oh but get yourself a drink if you want to."

Beth took a moment to look around. Woman that she was, she could not suppress a spark of curiosity to see what had been changed in the room that still harboured memories of childhood. Finally she sank down on a wicker chair and looked at her husband for the first time. "Thanks, I don't want a drink. You said in the telegram that you'd had an accident?"

"Ok, if you want to know, I was out with the local hunt, last outing of the season. We'd just had a sighting of Freddy. The field took off. Some youngster or other swerved in front of Hockey. Hockey bucked and threw me alongside Far Goose Spinney. Result, one badly buggered leg. Sure you won't have a drink?"

"No Saul, I said, I don't want a drink. I just want to know why you've dragged me out here, and then I want to get right back to London."

"Ah! Do I detect some urgency? Is there another party in the picture perhaps?"

The room suddenly felt stifling so that Beth fished in her bag for the handkerchief that she kept drenched in cologne. "If there was, that would be none of your business. Please tell me what this is all about, or I'm turning right round."

"Ok so, I'm expecting someone who I would like you to meet. Her name's Hilly, and she's a duke's daughter. Pretty fair seat on a horse too, if it comes to that." Beth got up from her less than comfortable seat to stare down the drive. "I was never interested in your other women. Why should I want to meet another of them now?"

"Ah well, that's the thing, see. Hilly seems to be a bit keen on the old marriage thing." Beth turned back to the room to find that her husband was now on his feet, hands in pockets, familiar smirk on face.

"Oh, so your leg is now miraculously better, is it?"

"Really did have that tumble; maybe I exaggerated the damage. Did you hear what I said?"

"Don't tell me you're actually asking me for my blessing?"

"No dear girl." As he started to mix another drink. "I want a divorce, and Hilly says it has to be me who divorces you. So we thought you might oblige by giving us grounds."

"Why should I give this Hilly anything?"

"Ok, good point. Of course it's me who you'd be obliging, and as the lady seems to be in a bit of a hurry I'd naturally want to see you right on the money – all expenses paid plus a little bit on top for yourself."

In the days to come, Beth would look back on the scene and wonder if her response would have been different had all of this taken place before the trauma of Harrow. Fists balled, small chin thrust out, she took a step towards Saul. She was about to tell her husband exactly what he could do with his proposition. Her mouth was actually agape when the door swung open to admit a big-boned woman cradling several yards of tricolour flag. "Ah ha! So you must be the little wifey. So sorry I wasn't here when you arrived but I've been scouring the attics for this thing. His master's orders, he insists we should be flying the Union Jack ahead of the coronation. I'm Hilly, by the way."

Embarrassed her mouth was still open, Beth retreated to her chair, assuming her best belligerent stare. At her back a sudden gust of rain spattered the window. Abstractedly Beth noticed the temperature had plummeted since her arrival. The woman called Hilly advanced towards her, hand outstretched. Beth ignored the hand. "My dear, I know this must be, hmm, a bit of a surprise for you, but you see, we, Dyneston and I decided it would be a good idea to, well, clear the decks at one go. Now why don't you help yourself to a little drinky while we go and run this item up the pole before it rains."

Beth was too angry, too upset to wonder about her husband's sudden obsession with flags. It was to be another day some way in the future before she would find out about that, and from Hilly of all people.

Beth looked away, said nothing. As Saul Dyneston left the room he half turned back. "Won't be long. Think about my proposition while we're away, eh?"

As soon as the door closed behind them, Beth sprang to her feet. Glimpsing herself in the mirror she saw that her cheeks flamed with the blood of anger. For minutes on end she marched up and down the room, vaguely wondering what they had done with her nice furniture including several Tringham family heirlooms. Finally, murmuring "Damn you both!" she pulled up next the telephone. She rang the taxi firm that had brought her to the Manor House. Because of the weather, she was told, there might be a delay. She flopped back on to her chair to wait.

Beth had no notion of how long she sat there, mutinous thoughts chasing round her head. Her trance was broken – not broken but shattered – by a thunder clap that seemed to rock the whole of the house. It brought her reflexively out of her seat so that she was on her feet when the bellowed shout reached down to her from somewhere atop of the house. Instinct and familiarity told Beth where she must go.

Hilly was there on the second floor landing, leaning at an odd angle out of the sash window, her hair streaming with rain water. Roughly Beth pushed the other woman away from the window. In the same movement she heaved upwards on the sash. The sash was stuck half way; try as she might, she could not shift it. All the time Hilly was shouting and cursing. Her words made no sense. Much the smaller of the two women, Beth knew it was for her to exit the window onto the roof. She sprang at the window and managed to wriggle her body through. Perching on the streaming slates, she sighted Saul in an instant. Her husband lay supine on the sloping roof, half way between the window and the gutter. Somehow the flag had become wrapped around his body so that both hands were trapped in its folds.

Beth shouted back through the window for Hilly "To fetch …" but her shout was consumed by another explosion from directly overhead, so near that it rattled the glass in the windows. She tried again. "Hilly, God's sake, get the nearest sheet, roll it into a strip! Quick woman!"

Without waiting she collapsed her body on to the slates, hooking one foot over the window's sill. Instinctively she reached down for her belt before realising she had chosen not to wear a belt that day. She reached an arm along the roof, but she was two feet short. The bed sheet roll then hit Beth on the ear. She grabbed hold. It was long. She twisted it into a loop and flung the closed end down to her husband, aiming for his head. For a moment it looked as if the ploy would work and that between them the women would be able to haul him back to the window and safety. The throw very nearly succeeded as the sheet bounced and bobbled around Saul's head; but in his frantic attempt to free his hands and grasp his lifeline he must have shifted his centre of gravity. The slick-wet roof took him and he disappeared from view while still thrashing his limbs like a man possessed.

Two floors down, the women raced and jostled to be quickest to find what they knew they would find. Saul Dyneston lay on his back, staring up at the rain as it sluiced earthwards to form pink runnels around the smashed head.

In due time the coroner for the district would make a finding of "Trauma to the cerebral tissue with the result that the expanding brain had nowhere to go."

Beth and Leo

Leo Church clambered from the mooring on to the bank, there to await his guest. He was still getting used to the manoeuvre so that he staggered slightly. Looking down at *The Sally-Ann* as if seeing her for the first time, he wondered with a qualm just what his guest would make of his riverside home. And more than that, what would she make of Leo Church. After all, their only previous meeting – if he could call it a meeting – had been the stuff of hard-edged nightmare.

Despite the restraint of her moorings, *The Sally-Ann* moved to the surge of the incoming tide. Near to 30 feet in length, her best feature was her cabin, which had a dashing rake to its profile. More importantly perhaps, it was weatherproof, and provided him with the snuggest of billets. Indeed, "billet" was the word for his new home since the ancient launch had come into his possession courtesy of his boss and mentor in the organisation, the organisation being the Red Cross.

Following his failure to arrive in Liverpool to be interviewed by the governors of the crammer college, Leo had received a terse note expressing their disfavour. His friend Will had brought the letter to Moorfields, reading out the contents to Leo. Leo promptly forgot about it. He had more serious things to worry about; besides which, an inner voice convinced him that he was done with teaching for once and for all. Instead, and towards the end of his time in hospital, he had got chatting with a Major Hendy, late of the Guards, who was high up in the Red Cross. After quizzing Leo about practical aids that might help Leo in his rehabilitation, the Major had eased his way to offering Leo a job in one of the charity's drop-in centres. It seemed that male members of staff were at a premium. Female members, Hendy explained, were as dedicated as any, yet they sometimes struggled with the more abrasive customers, many of whom had been injured in the blitz or wounded on active service. No formal qualifications were required for the job, which accounted for the extremely modest pay; but what clinched it for Leo was the offer of *The Sally-Ann*.

Major Hendy could tell Leo little about the pedigree of the cabin cruiser which, it seemed, he had inherited from a rarely-met-with uncle, and which had already found its mooring on the Thames when transferred as part of probate. There was some vague notion that *The Sally-Ann* had ventured to the French coast and back as part of that valiant "Little Ships" armada that had helped to rescue over 330,000 French and British soldiers from the beleaguered beaches of Dunkirk, though possibly sporting a different name. Indeed it was put to Leo that if he still had the energy come the weekends, he might care to sand down *The Sally-Ann* to discover whether an earlier designation might be revealed.

The note from the hospital conveying "Miss Tringham's" message had arrived the very day that Leo was packing his sparse belongings before moving out of Will's flat and setting up home on the river bank. Leo read over the note for a second time before showing it to his friend. "What have you got to lose?" was Will's laconic response. So it was that by that evening's post Leo had replied, inviting Miss Tringham to meet him at *The Sally-Ann*. This indeed was his sole option since her hurried note had omitted any suggestion that they meet at Flood Street or any more neutral venue in London.

Was he excited by the thought of meeting up with a fellow casualty of October 8th? Leo honestly did not know. It might turn out to be an embarrassing flop; on the other hand it might bring some sort of catharsis. Intermittently since the disaster his nights had been haunted by the explosion that had drawn such a heavy line beneath his 25 years of life, the explosion itself followed by the anxiety that he might be losing some or all of his vision. During the days he stuck rigidly to the surgeon's strictures to lie immobile for a specified number of hours and not to raise or lower his head other than very slowly. At these times he mostly listened to the Home Service of the BBC, managing to block out the noise, the smell, the physical concussion of October 8th. Through the fog of memory he vaguely pictured the girl who had tumbled into his compartment as the Liverpool express eased away from its platform; yet he could not now put a face to Miss Tringham, and certainly could not have told Will whether or not she had worn a ring of any kind. Finally his thoughts condensed around a single object, fuelled by native curiosity.

Now with evening creeping on, Leo gazed along the towpath, still wondering whether he would recognise Miss Tringham. Whatever happened or did not happen this evening, the wretched business with EJ's bank was out of his head, at least for the moment.

The clocks of several nearby churches were striking six when Leo spotted a diminutive figure heading towards him at a distance of a hundred yards. The figure was female judging by the blue pinafore dress – he thought it was called a pinafore dress – and cream coloured top. Miss Tringham, if this was she, was glancing down to her left to check the line of house boats for a welcoming face. This she did without breaking step, yet there was something, thought Leo, something quite discreet, not a hop exactly, more the suggestion of a limp.

Leo started to walk towards the figure. Beth, for of course it was she, tried a tentative smile. They met in mid towpath. Recognition shone in both their faces. self consciously they shook hands. Then in a rush each started talking over the other so that none of the talk made much sense. At *The Sally-Ann* Leo jumped aboard first, reaching a hand up to his guest to help her over the wooden gunwale. Only once they were sat in the cabin and Leo was busying himself with kettle and cups did their reunion begin to relax just a little.

Beth was first to break the ice. "Mr Church, this is lovely. You have a lovely home here, snug, yes?"

"Just as well I don't have a cat. Wouldn't be the room to swing it if I had. Oh and please, it's Leo, not Mr Church. Tell me, how do you take your coffee? Sorry I can't offer you a biscuit – haven't had time to do much provisioning."

"Black no sugar, please. Yes, I'm for that. When you get through what we got through, the world seems different somehow, different, less formal. So from now on I'm Beth, ok?"

Leo poured their coffees and handed the mug to the girl sat at the end of the sofa. As the mug passed from hand to hand, their fingers touched. Sitting down across from his guest, Leo blew on his coffee, looking down with wrinkled eyes in a manner Beth would come to know as characteristic. "To be honest, it's still with me, the crash I mean; but I think I'm getting there. You?"

"Reckon the same goes for me." Beth faltered while looking around the cabin and out of the porthole window. "Perhaps we'll get back to that. First, will you tell me something about yourself? All I know about Leo Church – apart from the obvious – is that once you wore glasses and now you don't. Sorry if this is too personal, but it makes you look, well, quite different."

"Ok, so I'm 25. Only child. Father died when I was really young. Mother lives alone in the West Country, sadly beginning to suffer from dementia. I worked six years or so in teaching."

"Oh, where did you teach? Would I know the school?"

"Merelles, it's a private school, part of the Woodard Foundation. I'm not there now," he looked down. "Suppose you could say I got the sack, not that it was my fault."

"Oh no, but that's terrible." Searching for eye contact.

"It's a long, not very inspiring story. Might bore you with it sometime. Suppose I've mentioned it because it was rather a lot on my mind at the time of the crash and it's not finished with yet."

"Oh, that's awful." Beth looked away, replacing her coffee mug on the window sill. At the same time the boom of a barge's siren echoed eerily around *The Sally-Ann* while its wash rocked the little launch. After a silence she continued. "Of course, that is none of my business but, well, we seem to be dogged by coincidence."

"How is that?"

"Well, perhaps that's my long and boring story. You see, I'm married, well used to be married. Officially I'm Mrs Beth Dyneston, but at the time of the crash we were living apart in every sense. As I fell into that Liverpool train really the only thing on my mind was how I might end my marriage, how I might, well, start again," she paused. "And then my husband died."

"God! You poor thing. Do you want to tell me about that, or no, it must be private?"

"The irony is that Saul, my husband, got me over to our old home with just that intention, I mean, to end the marriage. He had no interest in what had happened to me in October; he was only interested in ditching me so that he could re-marry a lady with money, a lady called Hilly."

"So what happened?"

"That same evening there was a storm, I mean, a real humdinger. As the storm broke over my old home my husband was on the roof, trying to hoist a flag. He must have lost his footing because I next saw him rolling towards the drop. The other woman and I did our best to rescue him, but we failed. My husband fell to the ground. He must have died immediately."

Leo jerked towards her, arm extended. "That must have been terrible, but it couldn't have been your fault. Doesn't sound as if you could have done more than you did."

Beth again turned to the window, watching the wash of the barge gradually levelling out to a ripple. Finally she said, "That's exactly what I hope a jury will decide."

"A jury?"

"As I was leaving the Manor House, after the ambulance had left to take Saul's body to wherever it had to go, this Hilly yelled into my face, 'You killed him, and that's what I'll tell the police!'"

Leo leapt to his feet. Hands in pockets he began a pacing up and down the cabin. "But you had no motive? unless …"

"Unless I was after an inheritance, getting my old family home back perhaps?"

"But you weren't, and in any case it's only that woman's word against yours."

"That woman has money of her own – that's what Saul told me. So, you see, she can afford to pursue her allegations. And Leo, they still hang women who murder their husbands, don't they?"

"I'm not a lawyer, but is there anything, anything at all I can do to help?"

Beth smiled. "Yes, if as I fancy there's a loo behind that curtain, may I make use of it please? Your coffee was nice, but it's gone right through me, and after that I'll love you and leave you. I promised my mother a phone call this evening."

"Please, help yourself. Excuse me, I'll see you topsides." Resting a hand on her arm, he ended with, "Thank you for coming, for seeking me out. I hope we can do this again. May I walk you back to Flood Street?"

Back in her flat Beth found a couple of letters waiting for her. The letter with the postmark was from Jean-Paul, her acquaintance from the Bournemouth train; the hand delivery bore the insignia of the police.

Jean-Paul

Beth swayed as she juggled the letters between trembling fingers. If she were to sling the hand-delivered letter in the waste bin unopened, would the nightmare simply go away? And what if she decided to become a fugitive from justice? She certainly could. October the 8th had seen to that. She had read of cases where the intervention of some disaster had made it possible for someone to go to ground, to simply disappear, making it impossible for the authorities to catch up with them. But then, in her befuddled state she thought, perhaps they could trace her through her employment. Ironic wasn't it that her ultimate employer was no less than the Lord Chancellor of England.

Beth threw the letters onto her bed. Without knowing why she shuffled into her bathroom. Standing on tiptoes she could glimpse a sliver of the Thames, but the grey bulk of the river was of no help, so she returned to her bedroom to collapse on her bed.

Beth stared up at the ceiling. There was a patch of damp where the ceiling joined the gable end. She was sure the patch had spread since the last time she had noticed it. Perhaps it would be correct to report it to her landlord? But it had to be something more serious than a patch of damp to distract her from the letter gradually moistening beneath her back.

A ghoulish image weaselled its way into Beth's mind. Years ago she had been helping her mother to redecorate one of the bedrooms in the Manor House. The wallpaper stripped down, they had come to a layer of old newspapers. These mother and daughter had gathered together, ready for the bin, when Beth's attention was caught by a photograph of a pretty young woman smiling full-face into the camera. Reading the accompanying article, the face turned out to belong to an Edith Thompson whom, it was reported, had that week been executed by hanging at HMP Holloway. Mrs Thompson, it seemed, had been convicted of the murder of her husband, a crime for which her lover, a Frederick Bywaters, had equally been found guilty. Edith

Thompson's age had been given as 29, not that much older than Beth was now. Beth shivered at the thought, trying to suppress the image of hanging.

After what seemed like a long time, Beth got up and went through to the bathroom to dash cold water over her face and neck. A glimmer of reality began seeping back. Surely she was more sensible than that? The Thompson woman had certainly murdered, had planned to murder her hapless husband; Beth for her part had strained body and spirit to save hers. She took up the letter once more, ripping open the envelope.

* * *

Paul was waiting for Beth on the pavement as she walked up from the Underground. They shook hands and exchanged tentative smiles. "So you got my letter, yes? Forgive me but I was curious to find out whether you had managed to trace your gentleman from the train?"

"I did, but it's a bit of a long story."

"Of course, and I expect you are hungry, so let us go in and see what Pierre our legend of a chef has to offer us this evening. Plenty of time for talk."

Paul led the way through revolving doors and across the lobby to a corridor down which a door was open to what obviously was the French Embassy's dining room. The room was empty apart from one couple huddled in the far corner.

Paul chose a table in the opposite corner, and before he could do so himself he stepped aside to allow a white-coated waiter to ease out a pair of chairs. As Beth sat down she gave herself a moment to take in the atmosphere of the large room. It was clean to a fault; it smelled pleasantly of wine; but the wallpaper was definitely faded with what a more experienced eye would have suggested was a *fin-de-siècle* ambience.

"This is jolly kind of you, considering we hardly know each other." She took up an elaborately folded napkin and smoothed it over her lap. "If I tell you I'm not vastly hungry, that might sound rather rude."

"Please, you must have as much or as little as you wish." Paul picked up the menu which he proceeded to study with serious concentration. After some moments he looked up. "Okay then, I think perhaps I can recommend the herb omelette. I've had it myself, and they do it very well here. And to drink? Perhaps I can interest you in one of our Bordeaux clarets? I know there's a 1932 that's drinkable."

Beth's mind choked back the reply, "I'll have what you're having," on account of it sounding just too gauche for words. Instead she smiled an appreciative nod in time for the arrival at their table of the sommelier.

Small-talk followed until the return of the wine waiter. Beth was ready for the little ritual that followed, adjusting the angle of her glass slightly before pronouncing the wine to be to her taste. The waiter backed away with a *"Merci Madame, Monsieur."* In unison they raised their glasses in a silent toast. "So, tell me now about your companion of the train, if you please?"

Beth took a larger swallow of her wine, running her tongue between her lips in a nervous gesture. "Well, his name is Leo Church. He's 25, and he lives on a houseboat on the Thames. He is, or rather he used to be, a school master." She filled in more detail, much of which she had garnered on their walk back to Flood Street. Finally she added, "And amazingly he is not wearing glasses. One of the few things I remember clearly about the crash was his horn-rimmed glasses, but they've completely gone."

Musing, Paul offered, "That is most interesting." He was going to add to this, but just then the first waiter was gliding to their table, enquiring if they were ready to order their meal. "Ah yes so, *Madame* would like your herb omelette, and let me see, yes, I think I will have the steak tartar. *Merci.*" The waiter noted the order, bowed and headed away.

In the time that it took for their food to arrive, Paul told Beth something about his own work, about his family in France, and events that had brought him to England. Beth struggled to respond with intelligent questions, though a second glass of the wine helped.

Served with practised elan, their food was placed in front of them. Beth approached her omelette with caution. One mouthful was enough to tell her that what she had in front of her was the real thing, a treat for the most demanding of palates. Unfortunately a further few mouthfuls convinced her she would never be able to get to the end of the lavish helping. Casting her fork aside she started to get up. "Jean-Paul, I'm sorry. You see, I've had this letter and, well, I don't know what to do." The letter was out of her bag and dropped down beside her plate. "I'd like you to read this, but before you do you deserve to know what has happened, what an accident-prone woman you've got yourself involved with."

And for the next twenty minutes or so Beth poured out the story leading up to Saul's death:- The summons by telegram with its urgent pretext of disabling injury; Saul's proposition and the introduction to Hilly; the feelings that were boiling up inside her when the storm had struck. Half way through her recital, while Paul steadily chewed at his steak, barely taking his eyes off his guest, Beth drew a breath. She took a gulp of wine while leaving her fork impaled in her omelette. Resuming her story, she worked up to the crisis atop the roof of the Manor House before misting up with silent tears.

Paul started to rise from the table, but Beth gestured with both hands that he should stay seated. Instead, she was the one on her feet. "Oh gosh! I'm sorry. You don't deserve this. I'll be back in a minute. Give you time to read the letter."

In the event, it was all of five minutes before Beth returned to the dining room, looking calm and composed, makeup refreshed and cologne scenting her coming. At once she saw that both their plates had been removed, at which she raised a worried eyebrow. Paul smiled across at her. "No doubt Pierre will be sad that you were unable to finish his prize omelette, but don't worry, I sent a message to say that my guest had suffered a bereavement and was not feeling hungry. I hope this is to your taste, Beth, I have ordered sorbets and coffee, yes?"

"Oh thank you. That's just what I need."

"How do you feel now?"

"I'm fine. Thank you."

Paul unfolded the letter. "So dear lady, this letter informs me that police officers from the constabulary of Kent are coming to London in order to question you about the death of Mr Saul Dyneston. For this purpose you are required to present yourself at West End police station at 12 noon tomorrow."

"Do you think that means they plan to arrest me?"

"I am no expert in the ways of the criminal law in England, but no, I do not think you should assume anything of the sort."

Just then their sorbets arrived, to be shortly followed by a large jug of coffee, all courtesy of the original waiter. With a small jump of pleasure, Beth saw that the sorbet was blackcurrant. She picked up her spoon. Paul continued, "I really do not think you should worry; but of course it's a shock, the whole thing is a shock. As I see it, you have several choices. You can refuse to say anything, though I do not advise this. You can have a lawyer of your choice accompany you to the meeting, though of course that will involve a fee. Or you can have a friend go with you …"

"Or I can ignore it altogether, perhaps swap homes with Leo, Mr Church. It's funny, but after the crash it turns out both of us had the same thought, Leo and I, I mean. When the crash happened each of us was on the edge, each of us was running away from something, knowing that our lives had to change but not knowing how that could happen. Leo, he was in hock to that bank; me, I was desperate to get away from my husband. We each had the thought, we've escaped with our lives; now we can be free, start again with nobody knowing any differently, nobody knowing, well, us." Absently she spooned the last of her sorbet into her mouth. "We could, well, disappear."

Paul nodded his understanding while he poured coffee for them both, adding cream and sugar to his cup after Beth had waved both away. "Disappear, yes, I have known that to happen, but only in a case where a fraud on someone's insurance is planned."

Beth looked straight into the steady grey eyes across the table. "You are really saying that I have to be honest, honest and open, that I must answer their questions?"

"That is exactly so, my Beth. You must not hide away; you must be honest. I tell you this for two reasons. The police have their ways. If you try to hide or to evade, that will only create suspicion in their policemen's minds, encourage them to probe further, deeper. The other reason? Honesty is no more or less than the expression of truth. Truth is – if I have the right word – yes, truth is subjective; it lives in the bones of the person who owns that truth. And the special thing about truth is that it is to be found by someone who has looked into the void and come back again." He lent forward, focus intense, allowing drops of coffee to splash from his cup. "You Beth, you have experienced not one but two incredible traumas. First you are nearly killed in an accident over which you personally had no control. Next, and not long afterwards, you witness a death in the most fearful of circumstances. You know in yourself there could have been nothing, nothing at all that you could have done to avoid the first trauma in which your body, as it were, closed down in automatic defence; but as to the second, well, you continue to doubt yourself, yes? This is perfectly natural, though there are two different states of the mind, which are not to be confused with each other. The fear that we might die by accident or suffer a serious injury to our self, these are fears to which mind and body can adjust. But when they dropped those crazy bombs on the cities of Japan, what did the survivors do? They made straight for the rivers and the hills because instinct told them in their permanence those rivers, those hills provided sanctuary and the possibility to survive. But the more deadly fears are those that, may I say, touch the soul. Yes?"

"Go on please."

"Yes, I think perhaps of betrayal, betrayal at the hands of a friend; or indeed I think of the death of a loved one; or I think of exposure to the cruelty that lurks in the average human nature. Yet do not imagine we can do without fear, because fear is the sergeant major that keeps our faces to the front. *C'est vrai, n'est-ce-pas?*"

A silent moment before Paul gestured with the coffee pot. Beth nodded, and Paul refilled their cups. Beth bowed her head. "So, where do you suggest I go from here?" and with a wan smile, "Apart from West End police station of course."

Paul thought for a moment. "It is perfectly natural that hope is hard for you to find; but please, I assure you, lack of hope is not the same thing as despair. History tells us of the man* who rolled a boulder to the top of a mountain only for that boulder to roll right back to the bottom. What did that man do? Well of course he went back to the bottom and started rolling the boulder all over again. Why did he do that? Because to do anything else would have been absurd, and what is the opposite to absurdity, why of course, acceptance."

"So are you saying I must accept before I can hope?"

He reached a hand across the table to briefly cover her own. "That man and his boulder, of course they're a symbol of all that is best in our acceptance of life. We are only free, truly free once we accept there is no after-life, that we must deal with life as it comes at us. We cannot extend our allotted days, so we have to increase our awareness of our self and our surroundings by converse, but most of all by conduct. In your case Beth, I could say that you have a head's start. Your compass bearings have been shocked, your 'true north,' your North Star has shifted, but now you will see everything, family, friends, places in an utterly new light, as if you have been

---

* Sisyphus of Greek myth.

presented with a gift, a precious gift. Like your friend Leo who, it seems, has decided, has been enabled to throw away his glasses, no?"

Silence for a moment and then, "Will you come to the police station with me?"

Leo Emerging

A Saturday afternoon, and Leo Church stands on the narrow deck of *The Sally-Ann*, wondering how best to improve his quirky home, more generally how to shape his new life. As he walks to the rail, the wash of a heavy laden tanker slaps against the free board, flinging a fine mist of Thames' water into his face. He makes no effort to avoid the sudden baptism. Sun dances on the wave tops, and the stench of rotting wood is all around.

Along the towpath and staring across to the Surrey shore, he is just able to see the site of the Skylon, iconic centrepiece of the Festival of Britain, and to picture the Dome of Discovery with its spectacular portrayal of the cosmos. When school-mastering in that long ago life, he was given charge of a party of boys to visit the Festival. Most of the boys had been impressed, but Leo had been more than eager to compare the bravery of this statement to the world against the slough of the Thirties, that "Low dishonest decade," as the poet had christened it. And somehow the advent of a new young queen with the aura of Gloriana had added to the firming of a new spirit for the nation, a fresh self awareness, and self esteem.

At his back, Leo can easily catch the roars of the crowds as they mount to a crescendo then fall away behind the ramparts of Craven Cottage, home of Fulham Football Club for fifty years or more. When he first heard the roar he thought there was something atavistic about it, but as it has woven into the soundscape of the river bank, he listens out for it, finding it vital and life-affirming. Leo has never been to a professional football match; the nearest he has got is Pathé News' highlights of the Cup Final with Stanley Mathews weaving his magic through the Bolton Wanderers' defence. At Merelles and like establishments, soccer was scorned in favour of the fifteen-a-side game, but hey, he must add it to his to-do list, a visit to Chelsea's Stamford Bridge or even Highbury for The Arsenal … The list of things to do, discoveries to be made, the list, he ponders, is growing fast.

Leo grips *The Sally-Ann*'s guard rail in both fists, flexing arms and legs. The tanker sounds its siren to pass under Putney bridge. "So," he ponders, "how is the old Churchman doing in life's balance sheet?" As always, at the top of the list is his mother. Judging by his last visit to the West Country, Jeanie is enjoying a new lease on life. The symptoms of dementia have not gone away, but neither are they any worse. He is quite sure this has been helped by Mrs Hemingway. Mrs Hemingway had come for a weekend through the agency of Dr Owens, but two years on she is still there, accepted by one and all as "Jeanie's companion." Mrs H. – Leo has yet to discover her given name – is a refugee from the Nazi occupation of Vienna. She admits to being forty. In return for her board and lodging she busies herself around the house, gets in the shopping, and generally jollies Jeanie along. Much of their talk consists of non-sequiturs, yet this does not seem to worry either woman. All things considered, Leo is happy with the arrangement. He telephones his mother each Sunday from the public telephone box near Redcliff Gardens, and this seems to satisfy Jeanie's need for filial contact.

As for his new job, Leo is content that he is doing something that is actually useful, truly serving humanity, and something more rewarding in its way than listening to the drivel from the mouths of Spider Williams and his kind. He feels a warmth towards the beneficiaries of the British Red Cross, whom he thinks of as his personal clients. The capital has only recently dragged itself clear of the smog emergency* that paralysed so much commerce and killed so many vulnerable people through want of clean air to breathe. During this emergency his office has remained resolutely open, though for the whole of one week Leo found he was in sole charge on account of that smog. Yet that same smog has in a few cases converted clients into friends.

He thinks of Amy. Amy is a woman believed to be in her seventies, though she has never admitted to her true age. She is widowed; she has just the one son, who lives with his own family in New South Wales. Amy, who lives in Stepney, has relied on crutches for bodily support and locomotion ever since the day towards the end of the war when a flying bomb demolished half of her street. In the thick of the smog emergency one of those crutches suddenly gave up the ghost. Leo's office was alerted to the problem by Amy's neighbour, and the same night Leo fought and groped his way through the toxic gloom to deliver a new pair of elbow supports to the

---

* The compressed combination of fog and coal fires produced the smog that caused approximately 4,000 deaths in the Greater London area.

address in Stepney. He was welcomed much as Stanley must have been welcomed by Livingstone, and rewarded for his small feat of heroism by a relay of builder's tea with something extra warming in it. He now has a friend for life.

Not that all of Leo's clients are like Amy. Kenny B. is a regular caller at the office. Kenny it seems has been haunting the office for so long that no one can now remember what his original pretext might have been. Certainly there is no visible evidence that he lacks support, moral or physical. Kenny is an old soldier, a fact that spices each and every conversation as he leans against the Red Cross counter. Whether or not it is true, Kenny claims to have been a Guardsman who has served in more than one theatre of war. He has ferreted out details of Leo's former life and its privileged trappings, and in particular his association with the public schools of England, and enjoys taunting him about what he calls "Those shit-scared officers." His favourite line refers to an officer allegedly of his acquaintance who was known for abandoning his tank every time a *Panzerfaust* poked its snout around a corner. But Leo can now cope with Kenny, and will not turn him away.

Thankfully Leo can remember little about Harrow and Wealdstone and the 8th of October. He knows that when he boarded the Liverpool express the fog-bound Wednesday morning, it was with a sense of liberation. He was escaping from his immediate problem, the entanglement with the bankers; more than that, he was escaping from a whole world of prejudice and rule by class. He had just the one friend in the world, his friend Will Piper; but it seems now that his biggest friend is the future.

Following the disaster Leo's mood, his outlook on life has chopped and changed with the weather. While a patient at Moorfields there had been a fierce concentration on saving the sight in his right eye. His treatment and his care amounted to a regime. His doctors, his nurses stuck to the regime, permitting Leo to do nothing else. When not actually following the strictures of the hospital, he slept – he found he needed to sleep a lot – and between times he was read to from the novels of Dickens by a motherly volunteer. His own mother Jeanie travelled up from the West Country on two occasions, bearing crystallised fruits.

Then, came his discharge from hospital. There was a difficult gap in his life before his meeting with Major Hendy and the start of his job with the

Red Cross. For most of the time he had simply moped and mooched around Will's flat, quite unable to settle to anything. His friend, of course, was sympathetic, managing to get Leo out of the flat, once to see a John Mills' flick and another time to tour the British Museum; yet it was all pretty hard work for each of them.

It was in this period that Leo's mood had plunged, almost gone through the floor. It was easier to make light of the nightmares than try to analyse, to put into words. But inevitably and during the long reaches of the day while Will was out at work, sight, sound and smell of the disaster would insist on nudging his brain. Why had he survived with his life when more than 100 others had not? Surely there was nothing special about Leo Church that had allowed him to survive. And then, there was that girl in the compartment with him, a pretty girl with fine bones and fine colouring. Had she survived? He was desperate to believe that she had. Then, out of the blue, the letter had arrived, telling him this girl with whom he had this real if tenuous link, was actually alive, alive and talking, walking in the world. And more than that, she now had sat in the cabin of *The Sally-Ann* where he was sitting now, drinking his coffee.

Leo's experience of girls had been slight, of women, even slighter. He had never shone at children's parties, preferring to chat with the birthday-boy's mother or father rather than cram into an airing cupboard with a mass of giggling girls. When it became time to embrace the boarding school life, he found he was bound into a rigid way of life that strictly excluded contact with the fairer sex. Of course there had been dormitory japes and jokes about nubile women with super-sized bosoms and scant clothing, but somehow Leo had found it difficult to connect with any of that.

Increasingly now he has been asking himself the question, "Church, are you really a natural bachelor?" Each time and especially in the watches of the night, he recalls the little Scots nurse who helped him through the first weeks of Moorfields, and tells himself, "No, I'm not." And by stages the gamine features of the Scots nurse slide away to be replaced in his imagination by the classical features of Beth Tringham. When wishing her goodnight at the door of her Flood Street flat there had been a moment when, given the smallest sign or signal, he would have thrown his arms around her. After all, there had been no evidence of a ring, no hint of a boyfriend to compensate for the trauma of her husband's death. He reflected now, they had not really shared anything else he could really call intimate; yet Leo had detected a certain reticence as if she might have had much more to say about her private life had he had the nerve to probe for this. Certainly he could not deny he was attracted by Miss Tringham, so that now, staring off to the lights beginning to prick their pattern in the dusk, he thinks up a pretext for a second meeting. After all, they had barely touched on the miracle that had seen them safe out of the crash. He so much wanted, needed to plumb the question he had been asking himself, the question that survivors cannot escape.

Out there on the Surrey shore a pleasure boat is idling its way back to its home mooring. From a speaker amidships Doris Day croons about her "secret love".

At the Police Station

The desk sergeant greets Beth and Paul with a lugubrious expression on his end of the shift face. He points them down a corridor to a door labelled "Interview room 1." The room is empty apart from the heat. They have no idea what to do, what to expect. Beth's eye is caught by a garish poster on one wall, illustrating the dangers of swimming in the Thames. Abruptly the door opens to admit their reception committee, a man and a woman.

The lead officer waves them in the direction of a couple of cane-backed chairs set against the wall at right angles to the imposing desk. Beth sits perched on the edge of her chair; Paul sits back, arms folded, legs apart. They are informed that the meeting is about to be recorded.

"Interview with Mrs Beth Dyneston commencing at," the lead officer glances up at the clock somewhere above Beth's head, "12 08 p.m. Present are Detective Inspector Campbell, WDC Hicks, Mrs Beth Dyneston, and?" the Inspector arrows a none too friendly glance at Paul.

"My name is Jean-Paul. I am here at the request of Mrs Dyneston in the role of friend and observer. Should you need to know, Inspector, I am attached to France's embassy here in London. I am a French citizen, but I understand English well."

The Inspector sniffs, presses record again. "And Mr Jean-Paul, observer." Fixing Beth with steel in his eyes, "You are Mrs Beth Dyneston, aged 22, and you currently reside at the Mews Flat, Flood Street in the borough of Kensington and Chelsea. Is that correct?"

Beth nods her head.

"For the tape please."

"Yes, that is correct."

"Mrs Dyneston, I need to tell you that you are not under arrest, that you are free to leave at any time. Nevertheless, in your own interests, I need to caution you." He looks sideways to his fellow officer who clears her throat and head down intones the prescribed words. Like her CID boss, WDC Hicks is in civvies, though the wrinkled stockings do nothing for her. The black skirt covers her knees, while the matching jacket lolls about her shoulders, the whole ensemble suggesting a scarecrow on a bad day.

"So Mrs Dyneston, you were married to Mr Saul Dyneston until that gentleman's untimely death which took place at the Manor House earlier this year. Is that not so?" DI Campbell's question is not exactly hostile, but nor is it encouraging.

Beth makes eye contact with her interrogator. "Surely you already know that? Yes, I am Saul's widow."

"Is it true Mrs Dyneston that in fact you and your husband were separated at the time of his death?"

"Yes we were separated."

"And would you say nevertheless that you could have had reasons to benefit from Mr Dyneston's death?"

Beth's hands wring together, but still she maintains eye contact with the man who is now sounding like her accuser. She raises her voice. "No of course not! What I mean is, my husband never discussed business with me. As for any will, I have no idea whether Saul ever made a will. He certainly never gave me anything while he was alive, so I'll be amazed if he has given me anything now that he's dead."

The detective from the county constabulary allows the tape to spool on in silence while he locks his gaze with Beth. He continues with, "So, may we take you back to the evening of Mr Dyneston's death. Tell us if you will the sequence of events that led up to the, hmm, accident."

Beth produces a handkerchief from the sleeve of her blouse and wafts it in front of her face. "Saul sent me a telegram to say that he needed to see me urgently, and could I travel down to the Manor House. It turned out he was after a quick divorce so that he could get married again."

"To Miss …?"

"Yes, to Hilly, to whom I was introduced when I got home, I mean, to the Manor House."

"Go on."

"So, we were in the middle of talking divorce when Saul broke off as he seemed desperate to raise the Union Jack up our flagpole before the rain came. He is, he was, always one for impulsive actions." She pauses before taking a hefty breath. "But then of course the storm arrived before he could deal with the flag. Hilly and I, we got on to the roof …"

"You both got on to the roof?"

"No, I got half on to the roof and I sent Hilly to fetch sheets which I made into a rope. It was all very difficult as the storm was right overhead. I managed to get the rope down to Saul, but he was unable to use it to drag himself back to the window because both his hands had got entangled with the flag. I saw him trying to catch the rope, but his efforts only led to him rolling further down the roof, and ..."

"Falling to his death?"

Once again the two detectives lock eyes with Beth, without following up the statement-cum-question. The silence is broken by Paul who leans forward to look directly into the face of Beth's interrogator. "If I may be allowed, Inspector Campbell, you seem to be assuming that Mr Dyneston's death was caused by a fall from the roof of the Manor House, but has the cause of death actually been established?"

Campbell directs his reply not to Paul but to Beth. "That of course is a matter for the district coroner, and as far as we know no date has yet to be fixed for the opening of an inquest. I should add, it is the coroner's responsibility to discover the cause of a death; his court is not concerned with matters of agency – in other words – who if anyone might have acted to bring the death about."

Paul persists, "Thank you. I believe I understand. So you, Detective Inspector, you are acting much as an investigating magistrate acts in my country. Is that not so?"

Campbell clears his throat with a haruff. "Well, I wouldn't know about that. What I do know is that you, Mrs Dyneston, have been accused of actions resulting in the death of your husband."

Beth half rises from her seat. Raising her voice, "And my accuser I assume is ..."

"I am sorry, Mrs Dyneston, but at this stage we are not at liberty to divulge that information."

"Well, I know it's Hilly because she accused me to my face. Inspector, you asked me just now what I might have gained from my husband's death; but why don't you ask yourself the question, what might Saul's fiancée have to lose as a result of his death?"

"As to that, my colleague here," indicating the WDC, "can confirm that enquiries are proceeding to track down the deceased's lawyers. You will appreciate that we are interested to discover the possible existence of a last will and testament."

During the interview, Campbell has been jotting down notes on a treasury pad. Now he breaks off the questioning to leaf through his notes. The small room steams with summer heat, and a fly repeats its efforts to escape through the shuttered window. Beth feels light headed. Eventually Campbell raises his head once more. "Mrs Dyneston, I see from my notes that just now you described the Manor House as your home, but surely it had not been your home for upwards of a year. Am I right about that?"

"You are quite right."

"Unless you still think of it as your home? Is it not the case that your husband may have committed your father to what the lawyers know as a 'fire sale'? Surely that must have been rankling with you and no doubt your parents for a little time? After all, am I not right in thinking that the Tringham family had owned the property over generations?"

Beth bows her head. "I have nothing to say about that, nothing at all."

Just then there comes a discreet knock at the door of the interview room. DI Campbell gets up immediately and goes to the door, but without pausing the tape recording. The door opens a few inches, allowing Beth to glimpse a figure in regulation jacket and cap. Campbell leaves the room, closing the door softly behind him.

What happens next takes Beth altogether by surprise. WDC Hicks who to this moment has resembled a sphinx, sashays around the desk and neatly seats herself alongside Beth. Briefly the women's hands touch. "Mrs Dyneston, Beth, I am so sorry if my inspector has been sounding, well, a bit hostile. It's only his tone, you know, and he always sounds that way. I've even mentioned it once or twice, but of course he is my senior officer."

Beth is uncertain just how to take this charm offensive. She half turns towards Paul, an eyebrow fractionally raised. Then she nods in apparent understanding. The CID woman continues, "I can assure you we are aware of what a difficult time you have had in the last year. You were in that awful train smash, weren't you? And now, so soon afterwards, Mr Dyneston's dying in such tragic circumstances. What I mean is, possibly your memory has become, shall we say, a bit tangled? I would perfectly understand if you were, shall we say, relaxed to see your estranged husband rolling down to his death, no?"

Beth jumps to her feat, hands balled into fists. "For heaven's sake, I tried to save the wretched man's life, didn't I?!"

The door reopens and DI Campbell returns to seat himself behind his desk. WDC Hicks scuttles back to her own seat. The fly continues to seek its freedom.

"So Mrs Dyneston, I don't think we can get any further today. Thank you for attending West End police station. You are quite free to leave these premises, but should you decide for any reason to change your current address or to travel abroad, this authority must be informed immediately. Is that understood? And, interview terminated at 12.55 p.m."

As Beth and Paul exit the interview room and head for light and fresh air, any casual observer can see the anger set in the bones of the girl's face. "Do they really think that I am capable …" Paul touches her arm as much as to say, "Save it for later perhaps."

Sat down on either side of a window table in Lyons Corner House, they order a pot of Indian tea. While they wait, Paul stretches back and smiles. He appears the picture of calm and relaxation. "Do you know, I really do not think you should worry, my Beth. Even if they believe that you killed your husband – which I really feel is unlikely – then we can easily convince a lawyer that the good inspector was out of order by leaving his tape running without recording the fact that he was leaving the room. I do not know whether that was intentional – how do you say, a ruse – or whether it was just a lack of concentration on his part; either way, I suspect it could go against them should matters develop. In fact, I'll tell you what. As soon as I get back to my apartment I will jot down a statement of what we have just been through. Then, and if necessary, my statement can be turned into what I believe is called a sworn affidavit, an evidential document. Oh, and talking of my humble apartment, I am daily expecting a visit from that niece of mine, the girl I told you about, young Cecilie."

Cissy

Cecilie or Cissy, as she prefers to be called, props herself casually in the entrance to her uncle's sitting room. She explodes with a theatrical guffaw, followed by "*Merde!*" Looking shame faced, Paul does not need it explaining that the girl's expletive is on account of the untidy mess in which he keeps his living space. The best he can offer in return is, "Dear girl, you are old enough to know that humanity is messy by nature, often ugly. And no, I will not translate because I suspect your English is rather better than you claim."

Cissy is 17. She is mollified to note that, poking out of the clutter, her uncle has the photograph taken in Paris on his last visit to the French capital. With the Arc de Triomphe as the backdrop, the photograph presents Cissy side-face to a sunlit world. The dark hair curls around her ears in a pageboy cut, and frames a face which sparkles with mischief from every vibrant pore. Her expression suggests she cannot wait to find out what will happen next in life.

Cissy is the younger of two daughters born to Paul's sister Claudine. She was born and has ever since lived in the 13th *arrondissement* of the French capital. She was three years old when war broke out in 1939, claiming her father's life within a year. For the duration of the occupation her mother doggedly succeeded in two things, earning subsistence for herself and her two children through her skills as a seamstress, and by keeping her head down. It was only towards the end, when liberation was in sight, that the second blow had struck the family, threatening to send Claudine's sanity spinning out of control.

Of all things, this had happened on the 25th of August, 1944, the day on which Allied troops had entered Paris. Cissy's older sister, Berte, had joined a large crowd of Parisians cheering on the liberating soldiers. A platoon of the hated enemy, marooned in their broken down *Kübelwagen*, came under attack from Parisians firing stones and whole lumps of *pavé*. One of those stones had missed its intended target, hitting Berte a heavy blow directly above her right eye. The eye was lost. For weeks it seemed she would retain perfect sight in the undamaged eye. Then, following the end of hostilities it was discovered that damage had been done to the optic nerve, and that Berte, by now aged 15, was likely to have only limited vision for the rest of her life. And thus it was that Cissy had grown up somewhat in the shadow of her sister, responsible for a variety of chores including constant tidying of rooms, thus enabling Berte to locate whatever she might have mislaid.

Now Cissy sets about her uncle's mess, not even pausing to unpack her valise or wait for the coffee brewing in the galley kitchen. While she directs her whirlwind to each corner of the room, Paul looks on in tame submission, doing his best to hide behind the ghost of a smile. Her onslaught completed, at least for the moment, Cissy flops to the floor and executes a dozen perfect press-ups, "To bring more of me to the surface," as she explains to her uncle. Her uninhibited exercise raises still more dust from the carpet, so that she immediately goes again for the vacuum cleaner. At last she comes to a rest in the middle of the room, hands on hips. "I suppose that will have to do. I think that coffee's ready, Paul."

Paul now prepares their coffee. He may not be able to keep his home tidy, but he does understand the reverence of true coffee-making. They sit, one either end of the settee. "*Santé!*" "*Salut!*" Cissy responds. "If I achieve nothing else in *Grande Bretagne* I vow to convert the island's coffee drinking habits. People here know all about tea, whether it comes from China, from India, from God knows where in their vast empire, but coffee? No, *mon Dieu!* Do you know, they market the essence in liquid form. A bottle costs almost nothing; the taste is abominable. *Alors*, the chance to show the world they are still a martial nation is not lost, because the bottle bears a picture of a sturdy looking Scottish guardsman. How do you like that, eh?"

"All right, the English do not know how to make coffee; but I think there are things you admire about them?" She hoists long legs onto the coffee table and ducks her head to her steaming mug to savour the strength of her uncle's brew.

"Oh yes, of course. They are beginning to appreciate champagne and other fine wines – especially French vintages – oh and there are a lot of other things including the big one, they never know when they are beaten. But enough about that, tell me, how was your journey, and how are Berte and my sister?"

Cissy noisily sups at her coffee. "*Alors, Maman est …*"

"Ah ah, English please."

"So, *Maman* is very excited just now because she has a new contract to work for Gallerie Lafyette in their sewing and upholstery department. Berte too has had some luck. She has a trial at the telephone exchange, the one nearest to home. She already knows what the board looks like, and she thinks she will be able to – what is the word? – operate, yes operate the system. Of course she is nervous as it will be her first job, but at least she will not have to move around at all."

"Yes, the eyes, they are something special. The chances of us seeing anything are very small. Light that may have taken millions of years to travel here from galaxies far far away has to first reach the eye and pass through a clear dome called the – I am not sure of the English word, but it might be cornea. The light is then bent to create focus. The light then passes through the lens, a clear inner part of the eye. When it finally hits a light-sensitive layer at the back, the retina, highly specialised cells turn the light into electrical signals which then travel along the optic nerve to the brain. It is here where these signals are turned into the images you see. The eyes really are incredible, the outcome of half a billion years of evolutionary change. They're good, but not that good, because there are creatures like bees that can see far more of our world than we can."

"Ooh la la! Now you talk to me about bees?"

"Well then, let us forget about the bees. You must know, I have much of sympathy for your sister. It seems to me she has not one but two mountains to climb. Without the vision with which she was born, she must learn to adapt in practical ways so that she can, hmm, impose her new world on top of the world that you and I experience from day to day."

"Which is just what she has started to do, I told you. But what is this other mountain she has to climb?"

"Ah yes, so the other mountain, that is to reach out to others without the use of her eyes. You and I, we, we speak to those around us by using our eyes. This cannot happen with the ears or the nose; but the eyes, they have that special thing, they can interact. So that will be the hardest thing for Berte, who will have to find other ways to, if you like, speak with the world."

"I know that she loves the photograph, the copy of yours over there."

"Ah, yes, photographs. Photographs, they have their power. The war, it would have lasted longer but for the photographs brought back from aerial raids. And then there were the hundreds of photographs and post cards brought back to this country by holiday makers *en* France, that helped the clever men and women who planned the liberation of our homeland, Cissy. They helped because it was important to choose the right beaches on which to go ashore."

"Do you think photographs are always good?"

"So, you read my mind. I was going to say that sometimes they can, hmm, mislead, because of course the print, the print is there for all time, cannot be changed. Somewhere I have a photograph of my cousin Marcel. At the moment this snap was taken he was unaware, and you could have said he was the complete – I think the English have the word – layabout – sour expression on his face, shirt unbuttoned. But then, a only a few weeks after that picture was taken, who should I see here on the Horse Guards Parade but Cousin Marcel, a proudly beaming member of *France Libre*, perfectly outfitted, knitted white scarf and all. So, we must be careful with the understanding of the photographs, yes? But getting back to your sister, I say bravo! What you are telling me is excellent news. Jobs are so precious, especially for you girls. During the war thousands of women found work in the jobs the men had been doing before their call-up. Since then the men have been re-occupying the market, making it that much harder for you women to compete." Paul gets up to refresh their coffee. "Makes me think of a young woman who by accident I have recently come across."

Cissy beams with curiosity. "Uncle Paul, please tell me more!"

"Ah no, it's not what you might be thinking. This young woman – her name is Beth – has, as they say, been in the wars. First of all she was caught up in that terrible train crash before Christmas. You may have seen pictures in *Paris Match*, yes?"

"I think I did."

"Then, if that was not enough, just a month ago her husband was killed in a bizarre accident, and now the poor woman is terrified that she may be put on trial for murder. She even has nightmares about hanging."

"You tell me the English still hang women?"

"Yes, I think there was a woman who was hanged during the war. Anyway, you're going to ask me how I met this Beth? So we met on a train going down to the south coast. I was on official business, you understand. We talked – this was before the accident with her husband – and two things came of our conversations. One was the amazing fact that she had managed to get a job at the first attempt, even if it is not exactly the kind of job, the kind of vocation that she might have thought of having at your age, Cissy."

"And the second thing?"

"The second thing, yes. Well it turned out there were two of them in the last carriage of one of those trains, the trains that crashed in the fog. *Mademoiselle* Beth seemed to be, no, seemed to have a responsibility for this other person, a man. She was desperate to discover whether he had survived, and yet she did not know quite how to find out about this. Anyway, before we parted, she promised to let me know if she had succeeded in tracking down the man. This she did. We met for a meal at the embassy and I learned about Mr Leo Church and their meeting on the Thames. The same evening Beth confided in me the summons she had just received from the police. She asked me if I would go with her to the police station, which I did. That was only this week. So, that is your uncle's story."

For the first time since bursting through the front door of the apartment, Cissy's face is re-drawn in lines of composure. "And it is a story the most tragic, *n'est-ce-pas*? Do you think this Beth and this Leo might get themselves together, might become friends, I mean?"

"I do not know because I have not met this gentleman, so I do not know what might attract him to her, her to him. But truly, I am fascinated by the, hmm, dynamic. I confess, I would like to meet Mr Leo Church. More than that, I would like you to meet them both. You my dear possess a certain *joie de vivre* that perhaps these two young people should catch. Maybe it's not as easy as catching the common cold, yet worth a try. Do you agree?"

"My uncle, I think you are asking me to, er, make the match."

"Oh, it does not have to be that way. These things happen or do not happen quite naturally ..."

"But they sometimes need a push?"

"I have a good idea of what it is to be the 'perfect English Gentleman.' I have not dined and sported in company with the gentlemen of *Grande Bretagne* for 13 years to be ignorant of their qualities. They are fiercely loyal to their caste, they have the *amour propre*, and yet they are like the slow burning fuse that needs igniting with the appropriate spark. I have even heard it said they are gentlemen to their boot straps – until they get to Calais."

Westward Train

Normally Leo has to work on a Saturday. This Saturday is different because the Red Cross office is closed for stock-taking and essential maintenance. He decides he will travel to see his mother in the West Country, pay her a surprise visit.

On the underground taking him to Paddington Station, he suddenly realises, "This'll be my first time on a train since October." The thought briefly racks the whole of his body in a cold sweat; but soon enough he is bursting out, up again into embrace of carefree summer sunshine glossing the summer dresses of girls.

At Paddington, Leo finds he is just in time to catch the 8.50 Cheltenham train, if he steps on it. As he gains the platform the guard is already unfurling his green flag, so Leo decides to play safe. He makes a dive for the last carriage. Only once he is aboard and hefting his weekend bag to the rack does he realise he has chosen the "Ladies only" compartment, the one without a communicating corridor; but as there are no ladies in occupation, he decides he can stay put with a clear conscience. What he does not expect is to be followed aboard by a second male passenger who tumbles in head down as the guard's whistle blasts out and the train jerks into motion. "Déjà vu," Leo thinks as the memory of Euston and the girl he now knows as Beth returns. Yet the memory is cut off in an instant as Leo recognises the just-in-time traveller. He has not seen him for at least three years, but right here, picking himself off the floor, is young Spider Williams, late of the Upper Fourth at Merelles Academy.

Instinctively Leo shoots out an arm to help the younger man up, but just then a jolt of the train propels Spider into a corner seat where he bunches his scrawny body into a defensive posture. "Long time no see, Spider."

Spider looks genuinely blank faced. "Sorry?"

"Come on now, you surely haven't forgotten your old school master? You can't have forgotten you were instrumental in getting me fired back then, back at the old school?"

Spider looks everywhere but at Leo. Finally his gaze rests on the panel housing the communication cord. "If you're going to hit me I've only got to pull that thing."

"Don't be damned stupid, Spider. I'm not going to hit you, especially as I guess you are on your way to Merelles' annual reunion, yes?"

"Ok yes, it's the Old Boys' weekend."

"Tell me, how is my old friend EJ? Are you still working for him and his, hmm, companies?"

"I suppose he's all right. Had a bit of a rocky period, but it was only his company that went down – limited liability you know – not him himself. And yes, I still do a bit for him, a bit of this and that, when he needs me."

Silence fills the small compartment while Leo looks out of one window and Spider the other. Eventually Leo fixes Spider with a stare the younger man cannot avoid. "Matter of fact, I'm pleased to have bumped into you today."

"Oh yeah?"

"Yes, because at long last I am able to give you an answer to that question of yours."

"Oh, what question is that, sir?"

Leo dwells on the "sir" for a moment before replying. "You were always fond of asking me, 'Would you rather be a spider or a fly?' So, I can now tell you, I would rather be the fly."

"How's that?"

"The fly is so much more mobile than the spider and its web. Of course, the occasional fly will always find itself caught in the spider's web; but most of the time eons of breeding teach the fly to stay mobile, to avoid the web, to live another day. Are you with me?"

"I don't understand why you're telling me this now."

Leo leans forward in his seat. "Ah well, Spider me lad, between you, you and EJ, you wove a bit of a web yourselves, did you not? But unfortunately for the two of you, that document EJ got me to sign that summer's day turned out to have no validity, to be unenforceable."

"Oh really?"

"Yes, really. I had my suspicions when I was reunited with the document in the bank, and I'm glad to say my suspicions were confirmed by a lawyer I consulted. Number one, my signature was never witnessed by an independent third party, by anyone; number two, it was obtained by duress, on the back of some sneaky lies, your sneaky lies, Spider."

Silence, and then, "Sorry about that, sir."

"So now, if you'll excuse me, I'm going to read my book, but do say hi to the old school, won't you."

The first stop is Reading. Spider Williams scuttles to the door. As he jumps from the compartment he explains he has just remembered he has to make an urgent telephone call.

* * *

Leo walks through the open door of Jeanie's cottage in the early afternoon. He pauses to inhale the familiar scent of lavender before launching a theatrical cough on the still air. "Only me, Ma. Come from London to see how you are doing."

A door opens softly and a prim little mouse of a woman emerges. "Oh my dear, what a lovely surprise! Is it Mr Leo?"

"And you must be the Mrs Hemingway of whom good reports have been heard. Is Ma, is my mother at home?"

"As your mother might say in her Scottish, she is away to her bed to have a little of her shut-eye, but why do you not go up? She has all of the day to shut eye if she needs to. I will be here if tea is needed. Have you had anything to eat?"

"Yes, had something before I left London. Tea would be good though."

Leo dumps his bag in the hallway and makes for the stairs, leaving a smile and a "Thank you" over his shoulder.

On the landing he knocks quietly on his mother's bedroom door. The knock is answered immediately. "Come in Dear. I heard you arrive."

Leo stands at the foot of Jeanie's bed, pausing to study his mother. Her face is flushed, but her silvery hair is freshly waved. She is sitting up, swathed in the purple bed jacket, so familiar to her son. Then he is around the bed and hugging his mother.

"So, how is life in the old homestead, Ma? Mrs H. seems in good form, but how about you, eh?" He backs away from the bedside, pulling a chair out from the corner of the room, the room that feels close, as if occupied for a long time. "Mind if I open this window a crack?" He doesn't wait for a reply but opens the window before seating himself at the bottom of the bed.

"Thank you, Dear. I think that I am very well." Jeanie wraps the bed jacket more closely around her narrow shoulders. "Now tell your old mother all about London, your job, your quaint little home. What have you been up to since I came to see you in the hospital?"

"Ok Ma, so, the most interesting thing that's happened is a visit from the young lady who was with me in the train that crashed. I think I told you on the phone that she had been in touch, no?"

"Don't remember that, Dear, but please go on."

"Well it turns out her name is Beth, Beth Tringham, and apparently her people used to live down in the land of hops and apple orchards."

"Tringham, Tringham, hmm. Yes I think there used to be Tringhams over that way," indicating with a wave of her hand. "Towards the border. Would I have met them, the Tringhams? What line is her father in?"

"Ma, I have no idea what 'line' her father might be in. What matters is, like me, she's a survivor."

The bedroom door opens to Mrs Hemingway, apologising for not being able to knock. The tray that needs both of her hands holds teapot, milk jug, sugar bowl, and a large plate of Nice biscuits. Leo jumps to his feet, relieving the companion of the laden tray, putting it down on the bedside table. He sits back down, leaving it to Mrs H. to pour the tea and offer round the biscuits. Leo comments that she has only brought the two cups; but the woman waves this away before quietly exiting the bedroom.

Jeanie holds her cup in both hands, sipping rather than drinking. "Survivor you say? But is she a pleasant-looking young lady survivor, eh?"

Leo turns his head to look out of the window to the leaves of the limes hanging limp in a drench of sunlight. He drains his tea cup and clatters it down on its saucer. "Pleasant-looking? Yes, I suppose she is really. Come to think of it, she looks a little like you must have looked at her age."

Jeanie sips more tea. "Oh well, Dear, I'm liking the sound of Beth Tringham already." She fixes her son with one of her looks. "She's not married then?"

"Not that I know of, Ma." He pauses. "Though, well, I suspect there might be a bit of a mystery there …"

"Which surely you should find out about if you and she …"

"Mother, there is no she and me as things stand, though I'm hoping she may come down to *The Sally-Ann* again next weekend."

Jeanie picks up a biscuit, toys with it, replaces it on its plate. "Dear, we have never, hmm, really talked about this, but your mother knows what it is to be a survivor."

"This is my father we're talking about?"

"Sometimes I have to try very hard to think what I did yesterday; but then I can remember the day the company manager came to see me to say your father had been killed, remember it as if it happened last week. You could say, I have been haunted by trains, first Gordon, now you. But you must not feel guilty that you survived. As I think of it, you survived for me. Perhaps Miss Tringham survived – for you."

Leo and Cissy

Leo stares down the length of the towpath to where it kinks out of sight behind a boathouse. He is straining his eyes for a first glimpse of Beth Tringham. Vaguely he has been wondering how to characterise Beth's walk. He has decided it is not so much a walk, more a skip. But the towpath remains stubbornly empty, apart from a tall middle-aged man in company with a girl – the man's daughter perhaps. Out on the river a put-putting barge whistles its progress down stream. Circling the barge a boiling mass of seagulls identifies the craft as a rubbish conveyor.

As they draw level, Leo nods to the man and the girl by way of a passing greeting, except that it turns out they are not passing but treating him to a frank examination. "Please excuse me, but is it Mr Leo Church?" The man has an open face with smiling quizzical eyes. He is smartly dressed for a riverside ramble, Leo thinks. "You see, we are here at the suggestion of Miss Tringham. Oh and by the way, this is my niece Cecilie."

Leo glances quickly at the girl, but long enough to take in the dancing eyes and the snub nose. "Is Beth, is Miss Tringham all right? It's just that …"

"Yes, yes," the man replies, "She was going to accompany us to meet you on *The Sally-Ann*; but at the last minute she has received the letter that she has an appointment to call upon an office of lawyers. She says to you that she is very sorry, but hopes you will excuse to have just us. She will arrange to see you again as soon as possible. But I am very rude. I should have introduced myself. I am Jean-Paul, attached to my country's embassy here in London."

The men shake hands. "I think Beth may have mentioned you. Didn't you meet up on a train somewhere? …" Leo is not sure how to continue, but the girl jumps in.

"I think your friend Beth must be very nice because my uncle he does not speak with all women he meets on trains. And I am Cissy, not Cecilie. She offers a slim hand to be shaken. A slender bracelet slides down her wrist. "*Enchanté* Leo!"

Leo looks from one to the other, putting on his welcome face. "But that's fine by me. Please come aboard, join me for a coffee." He jumps down on to the deck of *The Sally-Ann* and extends a hand upwards to help his guests down. He leads the way to the cabin where he sweeps magazines off the sofa to give his guests somewhere to sit.

The next few minutes are occupied with coffee-making and small talk. As the mugs are filled, milk and sugar added, Cissy jumps to her feet, intent on helping to hand things around. As she moves in the cramped space Leo is aware of her movement, not just a movement, more an impromptu ballet. Mission accomplished, Cissy sits back on the sofa, her mug cradled between her slim hands. "*Alors* Monsieur Church, I think you have a love space for a home, no?"

Paul glances in his niece's direction, a smile on his lips, then across to Leo. "I think Cissy wishes to tell you that you have a lovely space."

"Oh yes, thank you. Of course it's still quite new, but I hope it feels cosy?"

"Yes, yes. What I would like to know is, does your friend Miss Beth find it cosy?" Cissy asks.

Leo feels a surge of blood rising up to his face. "Beth? Well, she's only been here the one time, but yes, she seemed to like it well enough."

They finish their coffees. Paul gets up from the sofa, careful not to hit his head against the cabin roof, and replaces his mug alongside the kettle. "Mr Church, Leo, you will I hope excuse us. You see, I have someone I have to meet back at our embassy. But if you say that you have the time, would it be, hmm, impertinent to ask if you might spend an hour or so to show my niece some of the sights, as this is her first time to visit London, you understand?"

They part outside the broad sweep of Buckingham Palace, where this day's guardsman maintains a rigid stare a foot above their heads. As soon as Paul leaves to be swallowed by the gawping crowds, Cissy slips her arm through Leo's, urging him forward as if she knows exactly where she is going. "My uncle thinks I want to 'see the sights,' but I don't. Let us go to the movies instead. I have money. Yes?"

Leo raises an eyebrow. "What? On a lovely day like this? No, no, let me treat you to a cream tea. There's a great little café down there on the Embankment," pointing down the Mall, "where they serve the most scrumptious Cornish teas."

They walk. Leo walks while Cissy skips, humming something which he vaguely recognises as "*Auprès de ma Blonde.*"

The café welcomes them with a soundtrack of Guy Mitchell crooning through hidden speakers, harmonising with the chorus of chatter spilling from every corner of the place. As soon as they are seated at a table on the terrace overlooking the river, the first thing Cissy does is to go to her shoulder bag and whip out a pack of Gauloise and a neat little petrol lighter. Deftly she thumbs a cigarette from the corner of the blue pack, offering it to Leo. Leo shakes his head, his expression half-smile, half-grimace. Cissy lights up and sits back, a satisfied look beaming at him through the smoke. "My uncle, he does not allow me to smoke in the apartment. I hope you do not mind?"

"Well I guess it's your life, Cissy."

The girl's tongue flicks out, dislodging a flake of tobacco from her lower lip. "Pooff!" Accompanied by a pout of the lips, her exclamation sounds just what he imagines a Parisienne exclamation should sound like. Not quite "pooff," more "pewff." At all events it seems to sum up her entire attitude to life. "Yes, you are correct, it is my life."

A waitress in uniform of black and white with lace collar, jogs up to their table. "Sir, madam, I'm sorry, we've run out of today's menu cards, but I can recommend the cherry pie."

Leo and Cissy exchange glances. Leo says, "In that case I think we'll go for the cherry pie, two please."

"Will that be hot or cold, sir, with cream or without?"

With the slightest of shrugs, Cissy indicates she is not bothered either way. "Hot please, and with clotted cream." The waitress rips a page from her pad, and glides away.

Cissy flicks the stub of her Gauloise over the balustrade and into the Thames. "What were we talking? Ah yes, my life. So, I know what I am not going to do; I am not going to be like *Maman* or my sister, Berte. My uncle thinks of Claudine, my mother, as if she is some sort of heroine of the Occupation, but all the time she is simply a – I think the word in English is – drudge? Each day for her it is the same, sleep – food – train – work – train – food – sleep. And I can see very well that it is going to be the same thing for Berte."

"Ah yes, tell me about Berte."

"Berte is older than me. She is a little blind from an accident at the end of the war. She is being tried for a job at the telephone exchange, and each morning she leaves it to me to tidy up her bedroom. I don't mind this, but …"

Their cherry pies arrive. Cissy has been about to put another cigarette in her mouth, but changes her mind at the sight of the cream laden confection. Out on the water a yacht glides down stream like a giant swan. Cissy wastes no time. "*Bon appetit*!" Brandishing her spoon she spears through the pie crust, coming up with a brimming mouthful. A blob of the cream attaches itself to the end of her snub nose. For a moment Leo is tempted to remove the blob, but then decides against such an intimate gesture.

"It must have been hard for you all, in the war, I mean."

"Ah *oui*, yes, I suppose." She chews on her pie while gazing back to where the yacht is hoisting a sail. "But you know, perhaps we got used to it. The Germans, they came, they stayed, and we, we went on doing what we had been doing, surviving, keeping heads down, as you might say. At least our city, it was not bombed like your city."

"Do you think that was, shall we say, out of moral principle, or was it perhaps to keep safe a beautiful playground for their victorious officers and men to enjoy?"

Between mouthfuls Cissy repeats her "pooff," or was it "pewff?" "Who can say? I think I do not care for other men's principles. I wish to live my life by my own principles, just like that fellow in Algeria, my uncle is always talking about, the guy who plays football when he is not composing the novels, the essays and things.* That fellow teaches me I should live my life passionately, so that is what I will do. And you Mr Leo, you must do the same."

"Oh yes?"

"*Bien* sure!" Cissy leans forward. "Yes, yes, you should have nice women; you should marry a nice, a passionate woman; I think perhaps you should marry this Beth."

Leo raises a hand. "But hey, you've hardly …"

"Seen her. Yes I know, but it was long enough. She is, hmm, *une belle dame*, a fine-looking woman. I say she is chic, *chic comme une Parisienne*, and Leo, I

___

* Without putting a name to him, Cissy is referring to Albert Camus, French-Algerian novelist identified with the Existential school of philosophy, popular in post-war years.

saw into her eyes, deep into her eyes, and there is so much life in those eyes. As for her limp from that awful disaster, well, that will soon go – I am sure of it. And that train, do you not think you survived – for each other?"

Just then a young man with a fashionable crew cut sidles up to their table. He wears a pair of the new jeans fresh off the boat from America. He clutches a box camera which he points in their direction. The camera clicks discreetly. They are aware of the casual intervention, but think no more about it as their minds are still on Paris and the war, as well as cherry pie. Minutes later the same young man passes their table once more, this time sliding a glossy photograph between Leo and Cissy. Absently Leo removes the snap and tucks it in his pocket.

"Hmm, don't know about that, Cissy. It's all very well saying you will live your life according to your own principles, but what if the rest of us decide to do just the same? Surely we have to have rules common to all? I spent seven years being a school master, so I know all about rules …"

"And I too spent years living with rules!" Her voice is raised, her eyes flash. "Those rules meant curfew, meant rationing to our last potato!" She fixes his eye. They stare at each other in silence.

Sometime later, as the sun is dipping below the power station, they decide to make a move. Leo fishes in his pocket for a coin to leave as a tip for their nice waitress. He is hoping to find a shilling piece, but all he has is a half crown which he tucks discreetly under his plate. They leave the terrace arm in arm, without a backward glance. Had they looked back, they might have spotted the young cameraman deftly retrieving the half crown and sketching a salute in the direction of their backs.

With the Lawyers

Beth sits in the empty waiting room of Messrs Kinch Frobisher and Kinch, Solicitors and Commissioners for Oaths, whose nineteenth-century offices crouch some way down Chancery Lane, not far from the headquarters of the Law Society for England and Wales. She has not been here before, so that the sense of gravitas, of solidity and continuity impresses. The letter summoning her is in her hand now. The letter is headed, "In the estate of Saul Dyneston Esq.," and informs her she will be seeing Mr Frederic Kinch. Casting her eye to the printing at the foot of the note paper, Beth takes in that Mr Frederic Kinch is the senior, indeed the sole, proprietor of the practice. Vaguely she wonders what may have happened to Frobisher and the other Kinch.

Beth finds that she is ten minutes early for her appointment, so that she has time to take in her surroundings. The furnishings of the waiting room match the atmosphere of the whole establishment. In their stolid permanence they resemble the sort of pieces her Tringham grandparents might have coveted in the early years of the century. The chair backs are draped in sombre antimacassars; the alcoves harbour elderly aspidistras. On a table in the centre of the room magazines also of an elderly vintage hardly invite scrutiny. All the same, Beth picks up an edition of *Horse and Hound*, and leafs through its glossy pages with scant attention. A few minutes and the door to the waiting room opens. Standing in the doorway is Hilly.

Hilly is dressed as if her next appointment is a garden party at Buckingham Palace. The hat is not just a hat, more an elaborate confection; the perfume is so aggressive Beth can smell it from the far side of the room.

"Beth!" Hilly makes no move towards her nemesis, but crosses her hands over her handbag in a gesture at once defensive and instinctive. "Well well, didn't expect to see you here today!"

Equally surprised, Beth can only think, "Thank goodness there's no one else here to witness this coming together." Instead, she flings *Horse and Hound* aside, and jumps to her feet. "Bad luck for you then." She approaches the woman in the doorway, conscious all over again of her lack of inches, yet determined to front up to Saul's mistress. "Perhaps you're hoping I will walk right out, leave the field clear for you, but I'm not going to do that because I'm here by appointment. Just tell me, are you still asking the police to believe I killed my husband?"

Hilly has her red slash of a mouth open to reply; but at that moment a mature lady introducing herself as Mr Kinch's secretary, steps between the two women with the invitation, "Mr Kinch is ready to see you now. Would you like to follow me, ladies."

In the solicitor's first floor private office the two women take chairs as distanced from each other as is possible. The office is at the rear of the building, looking out over a grimy courtyard. The atmosphere of the room is muffled, the outer world silenced.

Mr Kinch half rises, stretching an arm across a piled-up desk to shake hands formally with the women in turn. He is a man of imprecise age – could be sixty, could even be seventy. The impression he gives is entirely in keeping with the ambience of his surroundings. The silvery hair laps his ears, while the skin of face and hands match the parchment documents spread around the desk. Mr Kinch is so much a part of the place that Beth vaguely wonders whether his home can be anywhere other than here. As for the voice, the voice squeaks as if in need of lubrication.

"Ladies, good morning to you. Do I have the pleasure of meeting Mrs Beth Dyneston,?" looking directly at Hilly.

Hilly bristles. "No no, that's Mrs Dyneston."

Kinch swivels his head towards Beth. "Dear lady, I do beg your pardon," sitting back and turning to Hilly. "So, you must be, hmm, Miss Hilda Doris Foster, no?" Hilly nods. "I believe this is the first time for me to meet either of you since the, hmm, unfortunate demise of my client, Mr Saul Dyneston late of the Manor House in the fair county of Kent, so please accept my sincere condolences on the occasion of his passing. Yes indeed." In response Beth's expression suggests, "What am I doing here?" while Hilly's can be read as, "Yes yes, can't we get on?" Instead each woman mouths "Thank you."

"No please, not at all. I can only think that it must have been a terrible shock for you, a terrible shock." Neither woman reacts, so he continues. "Don't mind admitting, it was a shock to me too. Over the years I have seen a lot of your, hmm, of the deceased. He was always in and out of this office, requiring my signature to this and to that. Hmm yes, quite a busy businessman was Mr Dyneston. Yes, but charitable as well. Do you know, earlier this year he was here, sitting where you are sitting now, asking me about the setting up of a trust for, hmm, waifs and strays. It did not go ahead in the end because unfortunately he and I found ourselves at crossed purposes as to the stated objects of the trust; but in the course of our discussions I was interested – I should even say surprised – to learn that he had himself started life in a children's home."

Despite themselves, the women share a quizzical look, as much as to say, "That is news to us!" What Hilly actually says is, "I believe my, er, Mr Dyneston left a will?"

Kinch immediately straightens his back and exits reminiscence mode. "Yes of course, and that is naturally why I have invited you here today despite the difficulty of the, hmm, separation. I am right, am I not, Mrs Dyneston? You and your husband had been separated for some time before his death?"

"That is correct, Mr Kinch, though we were not divorced nor legally separated."

Kinch eases a document file towards him, at the same time slotting spectacles on to his nose. "Well, whatever the circumstances my client clearly retained respect for you, Mrs, er, because I think we will find that he appointed you his executrix, along with myself, and that is one of the main reasons for me inviting you here today."

"Executrix? Can you please explain 'executrix'?"

"Why, yes of course. So, the executors of a will are the persons named as such in the testament, and whose job, whose responsibility is to give practical effect to the wishes of the testator, the person whose will is being dealt with, and where appropriate to apply for a grant of probate."

"Probate? What is that?" Beth is asking.

"Probate is the document that gives title to the assets in the estate, gives ownership to those assets, if you like, but only once the dear old tax man has had his dues."

"Yes, yes, but who gets Saul's property?" Hilly hurries her question.

"Very well, so ..." Mr Kinch begins to scan the paperwork in front of him. "I see that my client wished you, Mrs Dyneston, to inherit the silver soup tureen with the inscription 'VR'."

Beth bursts in, "But that's mine. It's been in my family for generations! It's an heirloom."

The solicitor duly notes the claim.

"Fine, fine. Let's not bother about the tureen. What about the main assets, the house and so on?" Hilly wants to know.

"After payment of all funeral expenses, debts, legacies and taxes, everything else appears to go to you, Miss Foster, once you are kind enough to produce your identification."

Hilly settles back in her chair, a look of smug satisfaction lighting her face. Now it is Beth's turn to jerk forward. "May I have a look at my husband's signature, Mr Kinch?"

The solicitor leafs forward to the final page of the document, at which point his complexion undergoes a rather less than natural change. The grandfather clock in the corner of the room ticks on solemnly while he stares at a yawning space at the bottom of the page. "Well now, to my surprise ... and my puzzlement ... it would appear there is no signature, no evidence that the document was in fact executed."

"Let me see that!" Hilly is again on her feet, staring down at the bottom of the parchment folio. She reads aloud, "Signed by the said Saul Dyneston ... in our presence ... Can you explain this to me, Mr Kinch?"

Kinch whips off his spectacles and peers at the lenses, as if hoping to discover some defect or obstruction. The grandfather clock ticks on. Then the glasses are back on the nose, and the lawyer is shuffling his file in a frantic search for a signed copy of the will. He fails to locate any such document, but instead turns up what he tells the women is a duly authenticated copy of Saul Dyneston's certificate of death. "Please bear with me, ladies, I am still looking; but in the meantime this document tells me that my late client died earlier this year, namely on the 21st of March. So there are two directions in which we can look." He unearths an intercom from underneath a pile of papers. He evidently speaks to someone in the outer office. A minute or so ticks by while Kinch stares at the ceiling, and the women stare at anything apart from each other. Eventually Kinch thanks the person on the other end of the intercom and directs a baleful gaze in between Beth and Hilly. "So, ladies, my managing clerk has checked the safe where we store our completed wills, and has checked the register. There is no will recorded in the name of Saul Dyneston."

"Could my, could Saul not have gone to another lawyer to complete his will?" Hilly challenges.

"Well Miss Foster, that is the other thing I have just looked into. My diary for the month of March contains an entry for Thursday the 19th to the effect that Dyneston was due to visit this office at 12 noon that day for the express purpose of signing his will. Clearly that appointment was not kept."

"Because he was laid up with an injured leg. I know that because he sent me a telegram, a summons really, to travel down to the Manor House," Beth explains.

Silence throbs in their ears. It is Hilly who breaks the silence. "So who gets his properties?"

The solicitor puts his hands together and sighs. "What I have just been able to tell you convinces me that Mr Dyneston sadly died without leaving a will, either here in this office, or anywhere else for that matter. This means that legally he died intestate."

"Meaning ...?" Hilly has a horrible feeling she knows what it means, but insists on it being spelled out.

"Meaning that the whole of his estate devolves, goes to his lawful relict and widow who, in the absence of any issue, that is children, I assume, means you, Mrs Dyneston."

Silence presses down in the room for the second time in the longest of minutes. Then Hilly scorches to her feet, the chair collapsing backwards. At the door she turns to glare at Beth. "Well at least we now know why you killed Saul!"

A Whiff of Sea Air and
A Chance Encounter

One early Sunday morning of blossoming sunshine finds Leo at the door of the mews flat in Flood Street. He is nervous because he is unsure whether his surprise visit will receive a welcome, or whether he will have to turn tail. His first knock resounds in silence, as does the second. He starts to turn away, only for the door to open wide.

"Wow! Hello! You're an early bird." Beth is still in her dressing gown that stretches its lavender length to a modest mid-calf. Her face bears no trace of make-up.

"Yes, sorry about this, but I thought you might like a day out at the seaside. You see, I've got a couple of tickets for the *Brighton Belle*."

Beth beckons him inside. "Oh gosh, and I thought you were one of those careful chaps who like to plan ahead, do things by the book. Now I find you're all impulse and devil-may-care." A bubble of laughter creases her smile.

"Of course, if it's not convenient, if you've got something else …"

"Come on, I'm only joking. I can do surprise, and it's a lovely surprise too. Give me, hmm, 20 minutes to get my face on, and we can be out of here."

"Great! And breakfast on the train."

They make Victoria and the *Belle* in its distinctive livery with five minutes to spare. They locate their reserved seats, but immediately turn back in the direction of the dining car where they order a full cooked breakfast and watch the suburbs flash by. Other passengers come and go, but without making them feel crowded out.

"Honestly, I didn't know how you would feel about travelling by train. Just thought, well, we've got to do it, yes?"

Beth reaches a hand across the table to squeeze Leo's. "Yes, you're right, and at least we're going electric this time."

"Yep, they changed to electric quite recently. Do you reckon you've got over last October? You're walking one hundred percent?"

Beth gazes out of the window at a gaggle of small boys, note books flourished, intent on their train spotting. Turning back, "Yes, I think I'm getting there …"

Beth is wanting to continue, but at that moment the waiter is at their table. The waiter is an elderly man, but as he whips the covers from their steaming plates he shows the dexterity of a professional juggler. He says, "Compliments of the chef, who hopes you will enjoy your meal, Sir, Madam. Coffee's on its way."

In contented silence they launch into bacon, egg and sausage. Soon the coffee arrives, and Beth takes charge. "Black with sugar?" Leo smiles a nod. "Yep, that's me. So, what were we saying?"

"Ok, so I have done one trip already. Yes, I went to Bournemouth to see my parents. Ah, and that's when I bumped into our French friend whom you met the other day, you know, with his niece. Tell me, how did you get on with young Cissy?" This with a coy smile.

"Oh well, turned out she wasn't interested in doing the sights, so instead we adjourned to that cafe on the Embankment."

"Would you say she is quite attractive in a gamine kind of way?"

Leo slurps coffee while thinking how to reply. "Yep, suppose you could say so. Between them, uncle and niece seemed keen to convince me how far ahead the Continent is in its thinking, and how far behind people like me are in throwing off the old order. Cissy was even wanting to quote some writer-philosopher chappy who I'd never heard of. To be honest, all I could think of was a trio of reprobate Fifth Formers at Merelles who launched a short-lived communist-type clique with the slogan, 'Progress – not reaction', though I kept quiet about that, feeling it was too un-British for words. But anyway, we were talking about Harrow."

"We were." Beth smiles.

"If I'm perfectly honest, it still wakes me up at night. Can't help thinking about those poor devils who were nearing the end of their long journey from Scotland, and of course the folk at the front of our train. If you really want to know, Beth, it fills me with guilt."

Beth squares her knife and fork on a clean plate. "Guilt that you survived, they didn't?"

"I suppose."

"But Leo, you are not the only survivor. I believe, hmm, I believe getting over something like that actually gave me the strength to deal with the ending of my miserable marriage – not that I was expecting it to end as it did." She leans back and fixes Leo with her best smile. "And of course, you and I, we wouldn't have found each other, and I wouldn't be sitting here now, looking forward to that sea air you promised me, would I?"

Their friendly waiter is passing. Leo flags him down to order toast. "Do you want to tell me about your marriage?"

Beth leans forward to prop her elbows on the table. "Well now, it's funny you should mention that. I'm not totally sure I ever was married."

"How do you mean?"

"Ok, so you haven't heard about my visit to the lawyer." Beth recounts the details of the meeting with Mr Kinch, not excluding the histrionics of her husband's fiancée. Their toast arrives and again Beth takes charge with butter and marmalade. "Anyway, the last thing Mr Kinch said to me was to let him see my marriage lines."

"Natural I suppose." Leo crunches into his first triangle of toast.

"Of course. He's not a lawyer for nothing; he's got to be sure with whom he's dealing. But until that moment I'd never realised that a marriage certificate is something I've never seen. So during my lunch hour I popped around the corner to Somerset House to ask for a copy of the registration."

"And?"

"And, I waited and waited, only to be told they had no record of any marriage between Mr Saul Dyneston and Miss Beth Tringham."

"Oh gosh, so?"

"So, as I was saying, I've got to wonder whether I was ever properly married. On that day there was no lead up or anything, and quite honestly I was in a complete daze. It has since come back to me that Saul was a bit, hmm, furtive in the way he dealt with the chap I took to be the Registrar, and it's possible that a bunch of money changed hands, though I can't now be sure."

Leo snatches up a serviette, brushes crumbs from his jacket. "About the will then – sorry, the non-will – have you any idea how the lawyers might deal with things if there really was no marriage?"

"Don't know for certain. Kinch was going on about something called the

'Law of Intestacy,' but I don't see how that can help me now. Don't see how it can help anyone if it's true that Saul was orphaned and brought up in a children's home."

"But that would mean waving goodbye to your family home, and anything else he may have left behind?"

"*Que sera sera*! as they say in Italy, whatever will be will be. I really don't care. I don't want anything from that man." This with an exaggerated shrug of the shoulders. "Don't you see, Leo, I'm free of it all. Till last autumn and the crash, life led and I just tamely followed, last in the ancient line of the Tringhams, and then as a kind of trophy wife, a mere possession. Now it's for me to decide what happens to me."

They fall silent. Across the aisle, a man in a suede jacket who has peeped around his newspaper at the note of vehemence in Beth's voice, resumes his cover. The last of their toast is left to go cold. Sometime later a sharp clamping of brakes and Beth grabs for his hand. "Ok, ok, I think we could be getting into Brighton. Nothing to worry about." But he keeps hold of her hand all the same.

Hand in hand still, they emerge from the station to a dazzle of light and a bustle of carefree humanity. Having recently read the popular *Brighton Rock*, Leo can't help thinking about the razor gangs, and picturing Pinky Brown as he slinks along the side streets with death, Rose's death, on his mind. But soon he forgets all of that, happy to give himself up to the frivolity of the sun-drenched day.

Straight away they make a beeline for the promenade, followed by the Palace pier. Some way along the pier they have to jump apart to avoid a racing trio of girls sporting "kiss me quick" hats. Beth's jump by chance lands her half way through the entrance to what turns out to be a fortune-teller's tent. She wants to apologise to the greasy-faced proprietress emerging from the dim recesses of her booth; but the woman is ahead of her. "Morning deary! You've found old Martha. Now sit yourself down on this 'ere stool, make yourself comfy like, relax, and give us your hand, yes?"

Beth finds she is too taken by surprise to do anything but comply, aware that Leo has followed her and now leans over her shoulder. "Ah, your genleman friend, deary. You going to cross my palm with a nice silver shilling, sir, or maybe two as you've come to see old Martha without an appointment like, and it's a nice day?" Leo fumbles but comes up with the shillings. The woman deftly pouches the coins, and in the same movement takes Beth's hand in hers. She takes a moment to stare down at the hand before pronouncing, "You have a strong life line, my dear." She stares some more while rhythmically kneading Beth's palm. "I see love, love and, hmm, a tall dark stranger – not very different to you, young sir," squinting up coyly at Leo from under her bonnet. "And yes, I see travel, lots of travel."

"Before I meet this tall dark stranger, do you mean?"

"That your hand doesn't seem to tell me, but there be trains in your lines, lots and lots of trains, but it's all good, hunky dory and Bob's yer uncle." Beth is releasing her hand, but the crone snatches it back. And yes," the woman puts on a more serious of her faces, staring hard at Beth's palm for moments on end. "Yes, I do also see flames."

"Flames? What do you mean, flames?"

"Can't rightly say about that. You see, your line, well it's gone a bit weird see, just a bit cloudy like." She looks up, "Perhaps if the gentleman wishes to …"

"Sorry, I'm cleaned out of shillings. Goodbye to you, Madam." Leo drops an arm down to Beth and they turn around to retrace their steps, looking back at the town and thinking about refreshment.

Back on the promenade they spy an open air café with one unoccupied table. An elderly gent with a newspaper under his arm is making his way towards the table with the look of a man intent on spending an hour solving today's crossword puzzle; so Beth and Leo take to their heels and manage to claim the table ahead of the man with his newspaper. Relaxing after recovering their breath, they look out to sea, inhaling streams of ozone-heavy breeze. The breeze makes a mess of Beth's auburn curls. She does not care; she is happy. They order platters of fried fish and chips, which they wash down with pale ale.

Lunch over, they spend time mooching around the town centre before Beth comes up with, "Hey, tell you what, I've always wanted to explore the lanes, you know, where you can look for a bargain antique. You up for that?"

Ten minutes and they are delving into the lanes. The narrow ways are thronged with day-trippers of all ages. They work their way backwards and forwards, peering into dusty windows, but without being tempted to cross a single threshold. Then of a sudden, Beth cries out, "Leo, Leo, see that!" She is pointing towards the rear of a display stand in the window of a down-atheel establishment. Leo follows her outstretched arm. "No, look further back. Yes, the tureen. That could almost be a twin of my tureen. Mind if we go in?"

The jangle of an old fashioned bell announces their presence, greeted by a young lad, a double of the Artful Dodger. While Beth makes straight for the article that has caught her eye, Leo asks the lad, "The boss around?"

The lad gives no reply, but lets forth with the shrillest of whistles. Very soon this is answered by the appearance of evidently the boss. "Good day to you, Sir, Madam. Damian Franks at your service. And what may I interest you in on this beautiful day?" His hands massage each other in time with his enquiry. "A nice piece of silver perhaps?"

"I, we may be interested in the soup tureen you have here. May I look at it more closely?"

"By all means, Madam. Take as long as you like. Beautiful piece, is it not? And solid silver of course."

Beth scoops the tureen into her arms, shaking it free of its coating of dust. The figures "VR" shine up at her; but to make sure she turns the piece upside down. With a finger she rubs at the underside before gesturing to the shop owner to inspect the faint scratch that her rubbing has revealed. "This item belongs to me. How did you get hold of it?"

Franks reaches for a dog-eared register before clamping eye glasses across his nose. A moment or two of casting back and forth between antique piece and register, and, "Yes, I have it. I purchased this fine item from a gentleman early in the new year, this year."

"Can you remember, describe this gentleman?"

Franks steps back to lean against his counter, and makes a show of massaging his chin as if in deep thought. Eventually he ekes out a rough description of Saul Dyneston.

"So," says Beth, "you have just given me an excellent description of my husband, who had no business selling something that belongs to me. I want it back, please."

The massaging of the chin increases in vigour. "Ah well, lady, there's the problem, see? Had it been our normal dealing, by which I mean, cash on sale, I might, I just might have been able to help you; but in this case the gentleman was so keen – I could almost say desperate – to get his cash that I'm afraid he twisted my arm, and we did a deal on the spot. Regrettably, dear lady, the tureen belongs to me." He opens his arms wide. "But I'll take a fair price if …" But he is destined not to do business since Beth and Leo have turned their backs as one, and regained the fresh air of the lane.

Back in London Town they head for where their ways diverge. With a skip in her step, Beth leans into Leo. "Thank you, Mr Church sir, I've had a marvellous day, and I've done so many things I've never done before."

"Like?"

"Well, like going on the *Brighton Belle*, like eating fish and chips outdoors, like having my fortune told," this with a spirited giggle. "But do you know, there's one last thing I'd like to do today for the first time."

"Oh yes, what might that be, eh?"

"I've yet to go to bed aboard ship!"

The longest day of Beth Tringham's life finally ends as the midnight chimes of half a dozen churches jerk her out of deep sleep. Just for a moment she wonders where on earth she might be; but then the slap of water against the hull of *The Sally-Ann* brings her fully awake. Down the length of her body she feels a sensation she has never felt before, a blend of heat and delicious pain, along with the feeling of security that comes from the care of love, the love of caring. To begin with, Leo had been hesitant, not helped by the cramped surroundings of the saloon, leading to bumps and self conscious apologies for bumps. Yet the tension, such as it was, seemed to vanish away as soon as Beth, with the softest of whispers, had assured him, "Don't worry, this is a good time, the right time." And what had followed had been moments of revelation and of joy, moments stretching in and out of time.

But then abruptly the pull, the grip of loving had dimmed as, unbidden, the image of a smiling murderess had pushed in between her eyes, along with the silhouette of a gallows, all of it mixed and confused with the implacable features of the CID inspector.

Beside her Leo's body stirs, emitting a gentle snore.

The Photograph

It is the following evening when Leo lets himself into Will's flat with a bellowed "Hi! Only me," as he charges up the stairs.

Will meets his old friend on the landing, clamping a hand on Leo's shoulder. "Hey, steady the Buffs, we're not on fire are we? Is this really the Leo Church I once knew, the guy who waited in the cold for me to let him in?"

"Sorry, sorry, sorry, but I just had to see you, to get your manly opinion on something."

"Ok, ok, but just let me turn down the gas on my spaghetti bolognaise – 'spagbol' to you – and you're welcome to share, if you've nothing better planned."

Leo collapses into the kitchen chair, fishing out a brightly coloured bandanna with which to wipe the sweat from his brow. "Go on then, you've twisted my arm. Don't suppose you've got a drop of vino going spare?"

Will does things with the stove before pouring a glass of wine from an already open bottle. "Think I'll join you. Obviously we've got heavy stuff to talk about." He pours a second glass for himself, and sits down next to Leo. "Cheers my old friend! So, what's this all about, eh?"

"And good health to you!" Leo takes a generous gulp of his wine. "Yes well, before I give you the back story, here I'm giving you 'Exhibit 1', so I can have your reaction before you hear anything else." Will takes the proffered photograph, twisting it round to get the best light. "So, what am I looking for?"

"Just describe, just tell me what you see there."

"Right, so this is clearly Leo Church sat at a café table next the river and, wow yes, a rather tasty-looking bit of fluff sat opposite you. Interesting. When was this taken, by the way?"

"Oh a week or two ago, but that doesn't matter – it's not as if we knew it was being taken. Point is, do you think it looks as if I'm mentally undressing the girl, or anything?"

Will studies the photograph with increased attention. "Wouldn't quite go that far. Mind you, it's better of her than it is of you. You do have a hand out towards her, and there is a hell of a sparkle in her eyes." He hands the snap back. "So, who is she? Tell me all about it, yes?"

Leo lets out a breath before swigging again from his glass. "Ok, right, well, you know about Beth, don't you?"

"Sure do, but of course you've been hiding her from me, haven't you. So is this young beauty Beth?"

"No, that's the point, it isn't Beth. As to meeting Beth, yep sure, I hope we can put that right. But I mustn't get ahead of myself." Leo takes a big breath. "Beth and I went out for the day just yesterday. We went down to Brighton on the *Belle*. We had a whale of a day. She was so happy as we were walking back from Victoria and well, to cut it short, she came down to *The Sally-Ann*, and we spent the night together – first time."

"Well you sly old dog! Not satisfied with one woman, you have to have a couple!"

Leo jumps to his feet, spilling the dregs of his wine, and setting to pacing the room. "No, no, no! You've got it quite wrong. Cissy – she's the girl in the picture – well Cissy was landed on me to entertain for an afternoon. She's the niece of Beth's friend Paul, Paul from the French embassy – surely I've told you about Paul. No, what matters is what happened this morning."

"Ok then, what did happen this morning?"

"Right so, Beth had to scamper off real early. She had to go back to her flat to change before getting to work on the Strand. I was awake, though I'm ashamed to say I pretended to be asleep for as long as it took her to dress. I've discovered, Will, there's something magical about watching a woman dress; almost as good as …"

"Taken as read, old boy. Go on then?"

"Well, you know how small that cabin is. As she was reaching for her coat from the hook, she accidentally brought mine down with it …"

"And what should drop out of the pocket but the photograph, the product of a young chancer working the terrace."

"Which I'd totally forgotten about."

"The lady took one look and …"

"Scampered ashore without a word, without giving me a chance to explain. All she left me with was the fraction of a stare, you know, how you look, hmm, how you look if you think you have seen a ghost."

Will stands to top up their glasses. "Mate, I can see how that happened, but look," slapping a hand on his friend's shoulder, "you mustn't give up, you know. Hey tell me, can you remember, what were you and the girl talking about when the snap was taken?"

"Wow let me think ... Yes I know, Cissy was telling me she intended to live her life passionately and that I should do the same, and bugger the rules."

"Well ok, there you are, don't you dare give up now."

* * *

The following weekend Beth and Hannah meet up at Victoria coach station, from whence the Green Line buses run. Their destination is the heart of the Chilterns; their aim is to complete a 15 mile circular ramble. The autumn morning is misty, yet the mist is soon pushed aside by warming sunshine.

Energetic, shot through with common sense, Hannah is the girl who was in the right place at the right time to scoop Beth up from the hospital following Harrow, and set her up in the mews flat. Their friendship goes back to schooldays. A year ahead of Beth, Hannah had bridged the gap of the years thanks to the girls' mutual passion for horse riding in general and eventing in particular. Each year their Christmas cards had featured their latest ponies, while Hannah had spent holidays at the Manor House. Neither girl had been that academic, though Hannah when not in the stables would usually be found with her head in a book.

Now in the autumn sunshine, the women clamber up hill to the trig point marked on their ordnance survey maps, to take stock of the landscape. There ought to be a green lane leading off to the west; and yes, there it is, and they plunge down to intercept the track.

"Wow, that's good. Can't tell how good it feels to get out of London for a change." Beth heaves out a huge breath.

"Right old girl, I can see that; but do you want to tell me what you're escaping from? Might there be a man involved perhaps?"

"Well, ..."

"Come on, I'm right, aren't I?"

"Ok, so I suppose we've never had secrets from each other." Beth brings her friend up to date with everything that has happened to her since Harrow, including her husband's death and concluding with the serendipity of Leo's arrival in her life. "Then just last Sunday he surprised me with a trip to the South coast on the *Belle*, breakfast and all."

"Nice work! Wish someone would surprise me."

They have been marching in step, but momentarily Beth with her shorter legs misses a step and has to skip to catch up. "Well, yes, we had a really super day in Brighton, and I ended up on Leo's boat – for the night."

"Oh wow, you sly young thing! And …"

They have made it to a stile, which suits both women – a chance to catch their breath and for Hannah to rescue her ponytail. They lean their backs against the solid timbers of the stile, gazing back along the route they have taken. Beth puffs out her cheeks. "If you're asking me, how was it in bed? Suppose the answer is cramped, cramped and a bit claustrophobic. Didn't mind that too much because it was more in the head than the body. We'd had a glorious day out, so that sleeping together – my idea, I should say – seemed the natural, the healthy climax."

"Ah yes, climax?"

"Right, and I know what you're asking. Problem is, I've really little to compare it with. As I was telling you just now, life with Saul only worked at all if it was on his terms. You could almost say that I shared his bed on sufferance, making myself available at his whim, responding in tune to his level of intoxication. I doubt I'm the only wife who has ever had to say that, but it was no sort of introduction to a caring, a considerate intimacy, to married life, to 'have and to hold' and all that. Do you see what I mean?"

Hannah twists the last strands of her mousy hair into its ponytail. "But there was 'caring and sharing' despite the cramped conditions, yes?"

"Oh yes, there was, and that's what makes the end of the story, well, so hard to take."

"Go on then?"

"Monday morning, as I was racing to get to work, and what should I stumble over but a glossy photo of the man I'd just slept with. He's sitting across a cafe table with a stunner of a girl who I'm pretty sure was Cissy, the French girl I mentioned just now."

"Ok, so what?"

"So what? Don't you think I've had enough to get through in the last year without being on the losing end of a tug of love?"

"This photo could have been perfectly innocent."

Beth hitches her socks over her trouser bottoms and starts to limber over the stile. "You haven't seen the sparkle in the girl's eyes, the rapt expression on his face, the arm thrust forward across the table. No, I'm sorry Mr Church, I know you are a caring guy, you have proved yourself a survivor, but this girl's not for sharing."

As they crest the last of the hills, a sudden gust of wind chases a curtain of rain into the valley. They plunge down the track towards a building resembling a scout hut. The hut is open, and proves more welcoming than its exterior would suggest. Toasted crumpets slathered in honey is all the women could have wished for.

They stretch aching limbs across rustic benches. Beth says, "Seem to remember, Hannah, you won the literature prize two years running at the old school, so perhaps can you tell me, who is Albert Camus?"

A Letter from Hilly

Another working week has come and gone for Beth. Her routine at the Courts of Justice continues just that – routine. The occasional day dream of escaping the capital and running her own stables and riding school, recedes ever further into the future.

Saturday morning dawns grey and drizzly. Beth makes herself a cup of tea which she takes back to bed with her. She feels no incentive to be anywhere other than bed; though in this she is not helped by recurring visions of police stations, and when it's not police stations, it's Leo and the ache of what might have been.

For distraction she switches her wireless on. *The Goon Show* does not hit her mood. She turns the wireless off again. She thinks about getting up to go around the corner to the telephone box to phone her mother, but finds she cannot summon up the energy.

Finally, distraction comes to her in the shape of the post, the second delivery of the morning. Beth has no idea who would want to write to her with anything likely to lift her mood. She will ignore it. Then a stubborn worm of curiosity gets the better of her, and besides this she realises she needs a pee, a pee followed by another cup of tea.

A single white envelope stares up at Beth from the mat. "Well," she thinks, "At least it's not a bill." Deftly she scoops the letter up, and in the same movement throws it through the bedroom door. In her bathroom Beth winces. The bathroom is so small it is hard to avoid a glimpse of herself from any angle. Now she sees that her auburn hair lolls lifelessly about her shoulders, instead of flowing with its usual vigour.

Back in her bed, mug of tea in hand, Beth studies the envelope. Her name, "Mrs B. Dynneston," and address have been hand-written in a neat copperplate. She is sure she has never seen this writing before. She rips open the envelope to find no less than three pages of closely packed handwriting. She darts to the end – the letter is signed "Hilly Foster." Beth feels ever so slightly sick, while knowing very well she must read what the mad woman has written.

The top of the first page sets out a post restante address, followed by, "In transit." The letter does not appear to be dated. On the other hand, it certainly gets off to a good start, encouraging Beth to read on.

"Dear Beth, Before you are tempted to chuck this in your bin, I have a confession to make and a sincere apology to offer. You see, I realise now, I have been behaving like a first-class bitch, and a dangerous bitch at that. I want now to apologise to you, Beth, in the hope that we can perhaps be friends, and help each other to come to terms with our shared loss. I have things to bring you up to date with, and a suggestion to make, but first, if I may, a little background if you will allow me. After all, neither of our meetings to date has actually helped any deeper acquaintance.

"If I may assume, Beth, that you and I are roughly the same age, there is no need for me to harp on wartime experience when we were barely in our teens. All I would like you to know about those days is, I hardly saw either of my parents from the start of hostilities to the end because they were taken prisoner and interned by the Japanese following the fall of Hong Kong, while I was marooned here in my own prison camp, namely a convent for girls tucked away in deepest Devon.

"I left the convent, aged 17, highly versed in deportment and Latin declensions and the Catholic Mass, but in total ignorance of just how the world wags, an ignorance that applied painfully to any knowledge of the opposite sex. I could however sew quite proficiently, so that I managed to earn a sort of a living working for makers of fashionable hats on Bond Street, while lodging with a maiden aunt in Highgate.

"Year by year my life trickled along in a pretty boring way until the day two Christmases back, when a girl at work and I, well we jointly won the annual sweepstake, the prize a day out with all expenses paid at the Epsom Derby the following June. And Beth, you have probably guessed already what happened next. Yes, as I walked by the enclosure to fetch lemonades for myself and my friend, I was – how should I put it? – waylaid by none other than your husband – not of course that I knew at the time that he was married to you or to anyone else. We girls, we somehow feel privileged to wear a ring following marriage, as if we're some kind of trophy, but the same it seems does not apply to men, curse them.

Anyway, after admiring my hat – it wasn't too dusty, though I say it myself, – dear Saul persuaded us to sit with him in his box. And besides that, before the big race and in my name he backed the winner at very nice odds, so that I came away from Epsom fairly rustling with pound notes.

"Well, after that I suppose, as they say in the books, one thing quickly led to another. By this last Christmas I had moved from Highgate to South Ken, to Saul's flat. Of course now I wish I'd stayed in Highgate, maintained my independence, accepting dates only when it suited me; but hey, there's no point in trying to work over past events; to do so would only be hurtful to you, Beth, to both of us really.

"So, I come to the most painful part of this letter, recollection of that terrible evening in March, the evening of the great storm. Beth my dear, if I may say this, you were truly heroic. You did everything you possibly could to save that poor man's life, and jolly nearly succeeded, only for me to accuse you of murder. I should add here that the autopsy established absolutely nothing that we were not expecting, and Saul's body was released for burial without much delay. There was no funeral service, and despite the death notice in the *Times* there was nobody to witness the burial at Golders Green. I say 'nobody' apart from myself, but Dawson, you know, that creep Dawson turned up, drunk as a skunk. When I think, Beth, of all those freeloaders happy to sup at Saul's table and down his booze, well I could weep! … But I digress.

"So, some days after our embarrassing meeting at the lawyers, I went back to see Inspector Campbell, and formerly withdrew my allegations as they related to you. You may expect to hear from the police accordingly, or so I was told.

"But Beth, thinking back to my disgraceful performance at the lawyers, which I blush to remember even now, I want you to know that I harbour no jealousy or resentment concerning Saul's property and your entitlement. Should you feel that you need my blessing, you surely have it. For my part, I have only the one tiny request, and that is you allow me to choose something from the Manor House, some little trifle with which to remember Saul. And besides that, Beth, I would like us to meet for one last time, to prove there is no lasting hurt between us, after which of course you will be free to forget all about Hilly Foster.

"I happen to be free in a week's time, i.e. next Saturday, so unless I hear from you to the contrary, I will hope to see you at the Manor House that afternoon/evening.

"With sincere regards,"

And the letter ends with a signature which conceivably reads "Hilly Foster," or it would have ended but for the following postscripts:

"PS Back on our black day I'm sure you must have wondered about Saul's obsession with the Union flag, given neither of us would have regarded him as any kind of a royalist. Well I think I may have come across the truth or some version of the truth one night when we were on the town, carousing with a couple of guys, fellow officers, who'd served with Saul in Italy in the last year of the war. Around midnight much the worse for Scottish wine, Saul suddenly turned maudlin, maudlin and then sleepy. As we were shovelling ourselves into a cab one of the other guys confided to me he had not seen Saul in such a state since the day the coffin of their commanding officer, draped in the Union Jack, had been trooped aboard ship. Much later rumours had spread that the CO's blood was on Saul's head, something to do with vital military supplies that had mysteriously been held up and unaccountably depleted somewhere far behind Allied lines. Evidently dear Saul had fixated on the sight of that flag ever after. Rather sad when you think about it.

"PPS I feel the need to come clean. I'm not really a duke's daughter, but I suppose you may have worked that out!"

"Forget all about you, Hilly Foster" – some hope! Beth thinks. Savagely she scrunches the letter into a ball, which she flicks over-arm into the bin at the bottom of the bed. The accuracy of her throw gives her a momentary sense of satisfaction. More than that, the rage that has been building through her reading of Hilly's letter, she now finds has kindled energy. Forgetting about her half drunk mug of tea, she dresses hurriedly. Talk of the Manor House reminds Beth she has not telephoned her mother for over a week, that she was going to do it today. She hunts around the flat for pennies; she races down the stairs, out of her front door, and around the corner to the box. Connected straight away, and after enquiries as to her parents' health, she launches into telling her mother of the possibility that she would be travelling out to the Manor House the following weekend, so would not be able to come down to Bournemouth until the weekend after that. This seems to spark an interest in Elizabeth Tringham. "Well dear, if you are going down, would you see if there's any sign, any evidence of my darling little Pembroke table, please? If you do come across it – it is an heirloom you know – it would be so good to have it back, don't you think?"

Back in her flat, Beth re-runs the conversation with her mother, pausing on the word "evidence." "Evidence" is a word she types 10 times a working day when preparing schedules to attach to the courts' dockets. In a flash she is delving into the waste bin and retrieving Hilly's balled-up letter. Impatiently she smooths out the pages into something resembling their original order.

At the Sign of the Phoenix

Leo wakes early. In waking, he stretches an arm out; but then he remembers. Getting up to look out at the day, he feels like going back to bed. The river has a dark and mutinous look to it, the Surrey shore indistinct, wavy with mist. His mind, his feelings resemble this morning's fog; he has yet to move on from where he has left things with Will. Just days ago the world smiled. No matter how commonplace the day's routine, it wore a patina of pleasure, a sense of anticipation; now that was gone, leaving Leo with the hollowness of loss. There was a time, not so long ago, when his folded away existence meant he was a hostage to nothing and to nobody, proof against hurt, proof against expectation; now all of that feeling taunts Leo like so much froth. "So, Church," he tells himself while dressing, "What you need is a very long, a very tough walk, after which, perhaps, you'll stop feeling sorry for yourself."

His walk takes him into the highways and byways of Chelsea. Almost before he realises what he is doing, he finds himself in Flood Street, not far from her door ... at her door. He knocks at her door, once, twice. At last he turns to go. Peeping out from the letter box, an inch of cardboard catches his eye. Clearly this is something other than private correspondence, so he removes the card which, it appears, has been torn from a corn flakes packet. The hurriedly scrawled note on the back reads, "sorry C, we'll have to do Hampton Court another day. I've had to dash off to my old home, down to Kent. Hope see you soon. B."

Absorbed in the message, Leo fails to hear the soft slap of footsteps closing his back. He is aware of Cissy only when sun-bronzed arms encircle his chest, and she is kissing the nape of his neck. "*Ça va Monsieur?*"

"God! Cissy, you really shouldn't do that! Some men might get the wrong idea. Here, look at this note from Beth – it's obviously meant for you."

Cissy takes the card between her two hands. "Ah yes, it was possible we go out today to see the sights, the Hampton Court Palace or perhaps the Madame Tussaud's; but ..."

"But it looks as if you're out of luck, as if we're both out of luck, doesn't it?" They stare blankly at each other as wraiths of early traffic stream through the mist at the end of the mews.

* * *

As the electric "caterpillar" speeds her south and east towards the bosom of the Weald, Beth asks herself again, "Am I doing the right thing?"

So much has happened to her in the span of less than a year, a year that has split her young life in two. One year ago she was the expendable half of a failing marriage, and she was drifting. She knows better now, but at the time she was in denial, wanting to blame herself, to look for shortcomings in herself that must have been responsible for the sad state of things. Could she have better blended herself with the extrovert excesses of her husband's lifestyle? Could she have steeled herself to be nice to his creepy friends? Above all, could she have done more to make them a couple, with shared interests, shared aspirations? Now though she realises, none of that would have made a jot of difference. Saul had married her – or not married her – as part of a greater speculation, part of a plan to get his hands on the Manor House and its land, all for a song. She would not have used the word a year ago, but now she has no reluctance to thinking of him as "That bastard who nearly ruined my life, while driving my father and mother into exile." Then, on a morning of choking fog, a morning intended for escape, her life had cartwheeled out of control thanks to a red light that had failed to penetrate that fog.

Beth counts the ranks of birches as they stream passed the window, brave autumn sunshine flashing lasers from their silver trunks. Part of that October day now seeps back in dream form. The shattering sound, the once-in-a-lifetime taste and stench of impact, this has been fading through the high days of summer. The one thing that has not faded, that may never fade, is the mantra, "I'm going to die." But of course, she hadn't died; more than 100 men, women and young persons had died, fracturing many more lives, some of significance stillborn, others humdrum; but she, Beth, had survived, survived for some purpose? Survived as a new individual, to see things, people and places, as if for the very first time, as explained by the Frenchman.

And leading on from this, she thinks about Leo. If there is a god to thank,

Beth thanks him for the coincidence that it was Leo with whom she had shared that last compartment of the Liverpool train. More than this, she thanks him that consciousness – ebbing and flowing though it was – had let her see that her companion was likely to survive like her, despite the shard of glass pinned to his eye. So easily her sole companion that morning could have been an octogenarian grandmother who had died of shock; but chance was, it was Leo Church who, for his own reasons, was also escaping a life.

Now Leo floods her mind's eye, his flop of blond hair, his slow smile and, yes, his gentle love-making. She has talked herself out on the subject while tramping the Chilterns with Hannah, but without convincing herself one way or the other. Was it possible she had overreacted to what she had taken as intimacy? A photograph could not lie, or perhaps it could? Something akin to panic grips Beth. As she knows of old, the next station stop would be Swanley. Should she jump off to get the next train back to London? And how would he be? Would he be pleased to see her, or perhaps? …

Finally she reminds herself she is on a mission, like it or not, she will have to see it out. Swanley comes, Swanley goes.

Beth gets off the train at the station she has been using for much of her life, the station for her home village and the Pilgrims Way. The walk ahead of her in the gloaming is a stiff march, though that does not concern her. She launches down hill, through the centre of the village, past the Horn, the local hostelry, over the brook, and on to the Pilgrims Way. She has not been to the Manor House since that awful day in March, the day of the thunder storm and Saul's accident. Her mind turns over the contents of Hilly's letter. Had she received such a letter a year ago, she would probably have accepted it, apology and all, at face value. Now she was not sure. Deep down, there was a nasty little worm of suspicion that would not go away. There had been nothing feigned about the woman's responses when they had met last at the solicitor's offices; so that words like "leopard" and "spots" nudged at Beth's brain. And besides that, she had yet to receive proof that the police intended to drop their criminal investigation.

A small rise in the chalky ground brings Beth her first sight of her old home. The Manor House stands where it has stood for four centuries atop the ridge, the ancient Pilgrims Way in its sights. The sight moves Beth. The carefree years of childhood unravel through her mind, only to be tainted again by the loss of her beloved brother, and by much more recent events.

So she is no longer sure how she feels about the old place. Could she ever live here again? She does not think so, and perhaps because of this she decides not to press on to the drive but to plunge off to her left to approach the house down the Dogrose Lane.

Half way along the lane at a point some 300 yards from her destination, Beth looks up for a closer view of the house. The evening mists are winding together, just starting to shroud the gables. At the top of the house, just below the roof line, the old nursery window stands proud in its dormer. She thinks she catches a flash of movement behind the glass. Was it her imagination, or has she just seen the pale blur of a face for an instant visible? Perhaps not; perhaps her mind is playing games with her.

A further hundred yards and the lane emerges from a dip. Beth stops in her tracks. This time it cannot be her imagination. She stares at a light that has just flooded the picture window next the front door. This is strange because she is quite sure that on her last visit she switched all power off at the mains. Then as she continues to stare, the light seems to erupt before her eyes, flaring into something sinuous and livid. She shakes from her moment of trance, and races towards the house.

Bursting through the privet hedge bounding the courtyard, her view is momentarily blocked by trees, so her ears tell Beth what she fears has happened, is happening. Somewhere in the house a window shatters, expelling a furnace roar that batters her senses. Panic grips Beth, but some instinct propels her towards the rear of the Manor House. The kitchen door gapes open. she plunges through, the sweet stench of ages flooding her nostrils. She gets as far as the staircase before a toxic surge of smoke and fumes forces her to her knees. She cannot breathe; a chaos of sound pounds her ears to an out of body silence.

Beth knows why she is here. She has come to recover her mother's much loved Pembroke table. Can she remember where to look? Last time she was here she is sure she can remember it being in the upstairs sitting room; but although she can just see the bottom of the staircase, somehow her body will not respond. Images flit through her failing consciousness, all jumbled together. Her father peeping around his racing page; her mother kneeling at the altar rail; Leo bending over her shoulder to part with his shillings to the fortune teller.

Painfully turning her head she spies Tigger the brindle cat, Tigger who seems to have been around the Manor House for ever, one-eyed, tail tall with predatory intent. But then, through her confusion, she realises it is not Tigger at all, only the copper kettle with its elongated spout winking down at her from the hob. Beth scourges her floundering brain. Surely there is a more important, a more urgent, reason why she is here. Someone else is in the house, someone who must be rescued …

She cannot move, though she fights for consciousness. She will never know how long she lies frozen on the stone floor of the old kitchen. Perhaps it is minutes, perhaps seconds only. All she will remember are urgent hands beating at her upper body, more hands dragging her backwards and all the way across the courtyard.

There are blurred shapes of bodies all around, bodies in frantic motion, and still this roaring in her head. Slowly Beth re-enters the world while choking the poison from scorched lungs. One, two objects swim into focus. The first is a body bending over her, blond flop of hair bouncing in the urgency of the moment. The other thing is farther off, attached to the lintel of the door, the tablet depicting an Arabian bird soaring into flight.